GREENLIGHT
STEVIE LEE

This is a work of fiction. Names, characters, places, and incidents either are the product of the author's imagination or are used fictitiously. Any resemblance to actual persons, living or dead, events, or locales is entirely coincidental.

Copyright © 2020 by Stevie Lee

All rights reserved. No part of this book may be reproduced or used in any manner without written permission of the copyright owner except for the use of quotations in a book review. For more information, address: authorstevielee@gmail.com.

Cover design and Interior Formatting by TRC Designs

GREENLIGHT
STEVIE LEE

For Mark

Thank you for the inspiration. I hope you're at peace now.

CHAPTER 1

As the only female K-9 officer the Arizona Department of Corrections has ever seen, I'm a little bit of a badass. But it doesn't mean I don't have to constantly prove myself worthy of my position. This is a male-dominant work force, and some consider women a weak link.

I work my ass off to be the best. Fortunately, I'm paired with the best partner a girl could ask for. Kody is a highly trained, eighty-pound German Shepherd, and together we bust more drugs than any other K-9 team in the state.

Every weekend, dozens of people flock to this desolate desert town to visit their loved ones in the state prison. Often, they see Kody and me as they line up for their turn behind the screened barrier, which allows him to jump up and sniff for drugs without touching them.

The Security Threat Group Unit recently received intel on a package coming through visitation today. I suspect it to be meth. That seems to be the trend right now. Whenever we find meth, the Zona MC is usually involved.

I pull my hair back into a neat bun at the nape of my neck. I want to make sure it doesn't get in the way today and it looks professional since I'll be interacting with the public. My uniform is a pair of gray tactical pants and a matching gray polo shirt. I've stomped into my duty boots but haven't bothered lacing them since I'll have to take them off to clear the walk-through metal detector at work anyway. My duty belt hangs over my shoulder as I grab my travel mug of coffee and hustle out the door. I try to wear my duty belt as little as possible. It's heavy from all the crap I carry on it, and my lower back hurts after a while.

I get myself clocked in and head to the kennels to get Kody harnessed up for a long day of work.

Kody's bouncing around his kennel, barking and whining in excitement. He and I are best buds after years of training and playing together. Happiness wells in my chest the second I lay eyes on him. His passion is contagious.

They say when you're doing something you love; you'll never work a day in your life. It stands true for me when I get to spend my days with this beast of a dog. To most, he's an intimidating sight, as he should be. But to me, he's my protector and my partner.

I grab a handful of treats and shove them in my pocket before letting him out. I kneel on his level and love all over him, cooing words of praise and encouragement. It's important for us to keep our bond and camaraderie to ensure we are the best drug-busting team this facility has.

When I can no longer delay getting to visitation, I snap on Kody's leash and collar and his demeanor immediately changes. It's time to go to work.

He's still excited, tail wagging widely, knocking against the backs of my legs as he comes to heel, but he's got his game face on and awaits my command.

The clicking of Kody's nails on the concrete floor alert everybody of our presence. It's instinct for people to want to pet the puppy, but we train officers to leave my dog the hell alone when we're working. A lucky few get a chance to interact with him occasionally, but only in the K-9 department when he's off duty.

We arrive in visitation fifteen minutes before they open the gates for the visitors. This gives Kody and me time to clear the area to ensure nobody can use the age-old excuse of "it must've been there before I got here." I also set up a half-circle barrier made of expanded metal. This will allow Kody to jump up and smell each person from head to toe. I'm sure it's scary enough with the barrier, especially for little kids.

Pro-tip: If you bring your children into a prison for visitation, don't put drugs in their diaper.

Kody passively alerts, which means he'll either sit or lie down when he detects drugs, keeping his snout as close to the find as possible. Even though his response isn't aggressive, the extra attention can be scary.

The morning starts uneventfully. Few people make it to the first rounds of visitation. I can't blame them; I sure wouldn't want to get up at the butt crack of dawn to drive to this small town in the middle of the desert.

The visitation officers have had to send a few women away for wearing revealing clothing. I can't imagine why any self-respecting woman would want to sit in a room full of men, who've spent years without the company of a woman, with their tits hanging out. My uniform isn't flattering at all, and I've usually got a baggy windbreaker on to hide behind even further, and I can still feel the eyes of the inmates boring holes through me when I walk into a pod in a housing unit. I've learned to ignore it over the years, but it was awful when I was a rookie.

In the back of my mind, I knew I should have expected some catcalling or whistles from the inmates walking through the gates my first time—maybe even an inappropriate comment now and then—but I never expected how lecherous some of the looks I'd receive could be. Some of these men held nothing back when it came to showing their interest in the female staff members. My skin would crawl, and bile would churn in my stomach from the uneasy way they made me feel. As I sat in my car at the end of my first day, I thought I was eventually going to get raped in a broom closet. It sounds dramatic, but I couldn't stop thinking about one inmate who stared at me with dead eyes.

It didn't take long, though, for my fears to ease. Walking around with false confidence and a no-bullshit facade helped me to gain not only the respect of a majority of the inmate population I worked with but even a rapport with some of the ones I had a tendency to interact with often. Many of them had jobs I had to oversee. Some of them had medical issues requiring them to check in with me so they could go to medical for treatment. Soon enough, I replaced my false confidence with genuine assurance.

    I chose this career because I thought I wanted to be a police officer, but when I became old enough to apply, there weren't any departments hiring. Somebody mentioned corrections as an alternative for the time being because it would be a great stepping-stone into other areas of law enforcement. The money and benefits were good, and they had positions available, so I jumped at the opportunity.

    On my first day of training, the instructors went over the different jobs I could do as a correctional officer without ever having to change jobs in the traditional sense. I could have become a locksmith or got a desk job keeping accountability of the inmate population while still being an officer.

    When they mentioned K-9, I felt confident in my decision to take a chance on this field. From that moment on, I made it my goal to become a dog handler. I still had it in mind I could carry the experience with me to a police department when the time was right, but after a short time with Kody, I became comfortable where I was and pushed aside any thoughts I had of leaving.

    With the visitation ingress clear of drugs and the partition in place, I watch through the narrow plexiglass window as cars pull into the parking lot. I've seen people dumb enough to take something from the trunk and try to stash it on their bodies before making their way inside. The ones who irritate me the most come to the window and look inside to see if I'm there before going back to their cars to ditch whatever contraband they intended to sneak in. Whenever this happens, I'm able to call our department's law enforcement, called the Criminal Investigations Division.

STEVIE LEE

I notice a woman dressed in a black knee-length skirt and modest pink blouse climb from her car. She spends a few moments smoothing her outfit and fidgeting with her hair and makeup before stiffly walking up the sidewalk toward the electronic gate giving her entry through the tall fences surrounding the institution. I've never seen her before, so there's a good chance her behavior is nothing more than nerves. I think most people are nervous to step foot in a prison for the first time. They don't know what to expect or who they might encounter. I make a mental note to pay extra attention to her when she comes inside, in case there's a nefarious reason for her apprehensiveness.

A visitor's first step is to check in with Sergeant Sullivan. She has them fill out a form, identifying themselves and the inmate they are here to visit. Next, they clear the walk-through metal detector while Sgt. Sullivan verifies the information on the paperwork. If they make it through both steps, they have a quick rendezvous with my handsome boy. The entry point is narrow, so we're able to control the traffic and number of people who enter. Once they make it through the points of security, the room opens a bit and has more of a lobby feel.

When the lady from the parking lot steps into the partition with her back toward us, Kody jumps up onto the barrier, takes one whiff, and immediately sits down. I snap my fingers and call for him to jump back up onto the partition, to confirm my suspicions. Sure enough, he sits right back down, nose to the metal grate at hip level, indicating the woman has drugs somewhere on her person. I make eye contact with the sergeant and nod toward the woman still standing in front of me.

"Ma'am, we're having trouble finding the inmate you're here to visit. The housing unit has said he's out on the recreation yard, so we've sent somebody to go look for him. In the meantime, you can sit here in the lobby and wait." Sergeant Sullivan directs the woman to a chair, where we can keep an eye on her while we wait for CID to arrive.

Investigator Kennedy arrives a short time later, after we've processed the last of the visitors. Sullivan hands him the paperwork with the woman's details. Sweat has visibly broken out on her forehead. She clamps her hands onto her thighs, trying to conceal the slight tremor.

Kennedy addresses the woman. "Ms. Jones, you could save yourself a whole lot of trouble if you'd hand over whatever it is you've brought in today." He flashes her a charismatic smile that gives me the creeps.

I interact with CID often. Whenever Kody alerts, they come in to investigate the situation and determine whether to press charges and prosecute. Kennedy is a good-looking man, and he knows it. His long, lean build is covered in a dark-blue button-down shirt, with the sleeves rolled up to his elbows, and a pair of fitted khaki pants. His dark-brown hair is short on the sides and combed back away from his face. He uses his pretty face to charm perpetrators, usually women in these situations, into giving up information. He also uses it to try to convince me to go on a date with him. So far, it hasn't worked on me.

The woman bursts into tears. "I don't know what you're talking about. I don't have anything. I'm just here to see my brother," she says through her sobs.

As if Kody understands the lady basically called him a liar, he lets out a quiet growl and paces around at my feet. Her eyes dart toward him and then back at Kennedy before she settles on her hands in her lap.

Kennedy chuckles and glances back at the papers in his hand. "Now, Melody, you mind if I call you by your first name? We both know that isn't true. Kody has never mistakenly alerted, so let's cut the crap and hand it over so we can wrap this up nicely and all be on our way."

"I'm telling the truth. I don't have anything," she says more confidently as she flicks her long hair over her shoulder.

I look at the floor and shake my head in annoyance. This isn't our first rodeo. Kody and I deal with this a couple of times a month. It's always the same. They think if they continue to deny it, we'll let them go. What they don't realize is Kennedy isn't a correctional officer. He's a police officer with the ability to make arrests.

"Ma'am, I need you to stand and face the wall. Sergeant Sullivan will perform a frisk search. This is your last chance to be honest with me," Kennedy says with much less patience than he had before.

"I've got nothing," Melody says defiantly.

Sarge pulls on a pair of gloves and performs the pat search but comes away with nothing. Kennedy places handcuffs on the woman and leads her out of the building.

"Lanier, follow me out, please. I'd also like Kody to take a quick walk around her car."

While Kennedy secures the drug smuggler into the back of his car, Kody and I begin our search.

"Hey, Lanier, I've asked for another K-9 team to come over to relieve you. I need to get your report quickly so I can make sure the charges stick. I need to take her to the county jail and have her booked in. I should be back in about an hour if it isn't too busy. Don't go home until I've gone over your statement with you," Kennedy says, all business now.

Kody and I finish our circle around her car, without any alerts, and come to a stop in front of Kennedy. Kody pants loudly as the early afternoon sun beats down on us. Kennedy wrinkles his nose when a large drop of slobber lands on his fancy brown loafer. Before I can answer him, he retreats to his car and drives away.

I scratch behind Kody's ears affectionately. "Good boy," I say to him, in the ridiculous voice everybody uses when talking to animals, and we go back inside to wait for Payne and his K-9, Ace, to take over.

CHAPTER 2

There's a river about half a mile from my house. I like to jog there on my days off. It's dry most of the time, but every once in a while, there's enough rain so the dam gets opened to let the water run through. I sometimes see mule deer if I run early in the morning or in the evenings around dusk. I'm getting off to a late start today, but there's always a possibility of seeing other animals too.

My run is uneventful. I saw a coyote run across the path about fifty yards in front of me, but that's common and hardly exciting.

I drain a bottle of water and head into the bathroom to rinse off and get ready for my lunch date with my best friend, Tenille.

I'm about as low maintenance as they come. I don't wear makeup at all for work, but I do like to wear a little when I go out with friends. A little black eyeliner makes my turquoise eyes pop. Sometimes I'll throw in some curls and leave my long brown hair down. I try to downplay my looks so much during the week, it's nice to feel pretty on the weekends.

I'm wearing my favorite jeans, an Eric Church concert T-shirt, and my old cowboy boots. They show off my curves perfectly. My T-shirt is tight enough to show off my thin waist and what little bit of a chest I've got without looking trashy. I like to leave a little to the imagination.

As I pull into the gravel parking lot at Suzy's, I notice the unmistakable puff of black smoke from a diesel as it fires up. A little tingle flares low in my stomach. I'm a sucker for a jacked-up diesel truck.

I park and watch as a custom Dodge 3500 drives through the parking lot and onto the road. It's completely blacked out, not an ounce of shiny chrome on it. I can't resist a tough yet sexy-ass truck. Add a little mud, and I'll fall at your feet. Dark window tint obscures the driver. I tell myself not seeing who was driving is for the best. He's probably not half as good looking as his truck, and I don't want the reality to ruin my fantasy. Tenille and I joke saying men who drive trucks like those are usually compensating for other shortcomings in their lives.

I don't know this from experience. I've yet to be with a man who drives a truck like that.

I grab my wallet and phone from the cup holder and shove them in my back pockets as I hop out of my truck. I can't stand purses. The only time I carry a purse is when my outfit doesn't leave any way for me to conceal a weapon, which is exceedingly rare.

I carry a subcompact .40 in the small of my back, tucked into a holster inside my waistband. I always make sure I wear a long-enough shirt so it isn't noticeable but still easily accessible if the need ever arises. I don't anticipate needing it, but I'd rather carry it every day and not need it than to be without it the one time I get into a jam.

It annoys the shit out of Tenille that I carry, but she doesn't see the evil I deal with every day at work. There are child molesters, rapists, and murderers, but I wish she'd stop to consider the guys who are doing small time for petty crimes but spend their days preying on the weak. They spend their days conning others on the yard as well as people on the street. It reminds me of those shows about people who fall in love with a convict through the mail. I can almost guarantee the con has at least one more person on the line. They won't stay locked up forever, and soon enough, they're back on the streets where they have a lot more freedom to take advantage of those

STEVIE LEE

who aren't expecting it.

I wish Tenille would carry as well. She's got to come across some shady characters tending bar. I know the local biker gang frequents there, since it's owned by one of their members. It's the same gang I busted for trying to bring drugs into the prison. I always worry one of them will wait for her, drunk, till the end of her shift and won't be willing to take no for an answer.

Tenille meets me under the covered porch of Suzy's, where she's smoking a cigarette. "Did you see the black truck when you pulled up? The guy driving it was fine! When I saw him jump into his truck, I knew you'd be all hot and bothered over the truck more than the guy." She rolls her eyes at me and takes another drag of her cigarette.

"I saw the truck. Sounds like I would've been hot and bothered over the guy too if I'd have seen him. Just my luck. Now, if you're done with your cancer stick, let's go eat. I'm starving."

We're seated at my favorite booth in the back corner, where my back is to the wall and I have an unobstructed view of the door and parking lot. Paranoid? Nah, prepared. Cautious.

The waitress barely walks away after taking our drink order before Tenille starts in on me. "Okay, so hear me out," she says dramatically. "I want to set you up with somebody. He's really hot. I think you'll like him."

I tilt my head at her in annoyance. "Tenille, we've been over this. I don't need you setting me up with guys from the bar. I'm perfectly capable of finding my own dates."

"Yeah, right. You refuse to date anybody you work with, and you don't go anywhere else to actually meet people," she scoffs. "Go out with this guy once. If you don't like him, you don't have to go out with him again. Maybe you'll get laid and won't be so damn uptight for a little while."

"Okay, so maybe I don't have the best track record meeting new people, but who needs new people when I've got a friend like you?" I give her my best smile, and the waitress drops off our drinks and takes our food order.

Once we're alone again, Tenille balls up her straw wrapper and throws it at my face. "You're so full of shit. When was the last time you got a good dicking?"

I grab the wadded-up paper from the table in front of me and smooth it out, keeping my eyes downcast. "Remember the guy I told you about who asks me out almost every time I have to call him in for a bust?"

"Shut the fuck up. You did not break your own rule. Why? You said he was sleazy," she says with disbelief while she stirs way too much sugar into her iced tea.

I stare at the sugar crystals swirling in her glass before my gaze reaches hers. "Well…" I drag my bottom lip between my teeth, trying to delay my admission. My lips break into a huge grin. "Just kidding. It's been a really long time, and I don't really want to talk about it." I fold my arms across my chest and tilt my head to the side, daring her to give me more shit.

We sit, our eyes locked for an uncomfortable moment before she finally speaks. "My heart breaks for you, my love. You can't stay celibate forever."

I take a deep breath in irritation. I should've known she wouldn't cut me any slack.

"Eh, a little longer won't kill me. I'll be fine."

Our food arrives, and we eat in silence for a bit. When Tenille can't take it any longer, she says, "I'm seriously concerned for your health. Blue bean is real."

I snort out a laugh, almost choking on the fry in my mouth. "*Blue bean?* Seriously? I don't think I want to know."

Tenille's features become serious. "Yes, blue bean. Google it. You'll start having actual pain if you don't get that taken care of."

A change of subject is in order. The state of my sex life is not the best topic for polite dinner conversation. "How's Ram?"

Ram is Tenille's… I don't know what to call him, honestly. The guy she sleeps with when he's in town? Her smash piece? And he's also the owner of the bar where she lives and works. I don't know the entire story there; she's purposely vague anytime I ask. He lets her live in the apartment above his bar, and in return, she runs it while he's away. When he comes around, they fuck like bunnies until he leaves again.

She picks up a chunk of her hair and inspects the ends, refusing to make eye contact. "He's good, I guess. Was here last week for a few days, but he had to take off. Said there was something brewing with the club and wasn't sure when he'd be back around." She drops her hair and makes eye contact with me. "Look, I know you don't really care about Ram. You guys are on opposite sides of the fence in my life, and I try to keep it that way. Just know he takes good care of me and let's leave it alone." She drops her silverware and napkin on her plate and shoves it to the end of the table, the rest of her food abandoned.

I do the same, my appetite gone away.

Tenille's features soften. "Have you heard from your parents lately?"

"Nope," I reply.

Of all the shitty topics we could discuss, this is the one she chooses. It must be punishment for turning the tables on her.

My parents hadn't planned to have kids. They were both college professors and loved their regimented lives the way they were. Then along came me, a menopausal mishap, who threw a wrench in the works. They figured they were old enough not to have to worry about kids anymore when I surprised them. They made it their mission not to raise a child but to raise an adult. I was to be seen and not heard and was expected to be respectful and mature. It was a cold environment to grow up in, and I couldn't wait to escape.

Much to their dismay, I attended a different school from where they worked and never looked back. I get a phone call around my birthday every year from my father, but that is the only communication we have anymore.

Tenille became my family when I met her by chance at a local coffee shop. I officially had the job at the prison, but my start date for training was a month away. I came to town early to find a place to live so I could settle in when it came time to focus on my new job. When I arrived, I stopped at a small coffee shop to grab breakfast and search through a local real estate ad.

I hadn't been paying much attention to my surroundings when I got there, a trait that would change drastically in the weeks to come, so I didn't notice there wasn't a free table. By the time I realized I had no place to sit, I had no other choice but to stand there awkwardly with a tray full of food in one hand and a cup of coffee and a newspaper balanced precariously in the other. Everybody seemed to glance at me but look away quickly, without making eye contact—except for one. A tiny girl with bright-blonde hair and big green eyes waved me over and invited me to sit with her. She helped me comb through the rental listings, pointing out places in good neighborhoods and crossing out the not-so-desirable ones.

Her quick wit and inappropriate sense of humor drew me in. She was kind to me when everyone else looked the other way. She was my complete opposite, but somehow we seemed to balance each other out. We started an amazing friendship.

While we're wrapping up lunch, my cell phone rings. I pull it from my back pocket and see "Restricted" on the screen. That only means one thing; somebody from the prison is calling me. "Shit, I've got to answer this. It's work." I jump up and head for the door to get away from the noise of the diner. I don't miss Tenille rolling her eyes at me before I walk away.

After I wrap up the call from the chief of security, I go to the counter and pay the bill for our lunch. It's the least I can do, since I'm about to bail on the rest of our day together. When I get back to the table to let Tenille know I'm heading into work, she's already gathering her things to leave.

STEVIE LEE

"Let me guess, they've got a new inmate they think has drugs up his ass, and you and Kody have to go save the day. This happens every time we try to hang out. Can't they call the other guy in and cut you some slack? Lindsay, you deserve to have a day that doesn't revolve around the fucking place."

I knew this was coming. I can't remember the last time we made it through an entire day without getting interrupted by somebody from work.

"I know, I know, but it doesn't change the fact I have to go. I've got to go change into my uniform and make it into the facility in the next thirty minutes. I'm really sorry to bail on you again."

I truly am. I wanted to sit and bullshit with her all afternoon and relax in a nice cool theater to watch a movie before it made it to DVD, but that isn't the way my life gets played out right now.

I've devoted myself to a job set on making my life hell. It takes up all my time, and when I get a quick break, I'm too tired to do anything other than sleep. On the rare occasion I get out of the house, my day gets interrupted, as it has today.

I can't even tell you the last time I've been out on a date. The only men I ever meet are on the other side of two rows of high fencing topped with razor wire. Unfortunately, most of them are wearing prison orange, and the rest are wearing a uniform matching mine. Neither profile is high on my list of dating potentials. I made the mistake once, and I'm not keen on making it again—the uniformed type, not the orange-jumpsuit type.

Shortly after I started working at the prison, I dated a fellow officer, Ryan. It started out fine until other officers caught wind of our relationship. Then it felt like there was always somebody up our asses, watching every move we made.

They picked apart any interaction we had at work, looking for anything they considered inappropriate to report back to our supervisors. We always kept it professional, but somebody always found something they didn't approve of. After two years of the bullshit, we decided it wasn't worth the effort and split up.

Then it was almost worse. Everybody made it their business to report to us what the other was up to all the time. Neither of us cared. Our breakup wasn't nasty or anything, just two people deciding to go separate ways. But people tried to fuel a nonexistent fire. I was thankful when he finally got a job with the Mesa Police Department and quit.

For the most part, people stopped talking about him once he was gone. Occasionally, a gossipy female brings him up, but I'm quick to shut her down. That part of my life is over. No more dating guys from work.

CHAPTER 3

"Lanier, we've got word the drugs you found were meant for an associate of Butch Hammond. We're certain this wasn't their first attempt, considering the excessive amount recovered. I'm willing to bet they started out with small amounts and increased it each time they got away with it. We've decided to have you search his entire pod and see what you come up with. I've had the captain assemble a shakedown crew for you. They're already waiting in the briefing room. Nobody else knows about this, so we're hoping for the element of surprise."

"How much is excessive?" I ask. Since the drugs had to be recovered through a strip-search at the jail, I didn't hear the exact amount.

He flips through a stack of papers on the desk in front of him, peering through the bi-focal portion of his glasses. "Looks like approximately a quarter pound of methamphetamine."

That's a lot of crank. "Do we know the value?"

He pulls his glasses off and sets them on the reports, then clasps his hands on top. His shoulders hunch forward. "Kennedy's informant told him that much goes for six to seven thousand on the streets. In here, done right, we're talking a minimum of twenty thousand. Probably more."

Kody and I have made quite a dent in the gang's profit margin. My chest swells with pride. This is what drew me into K-9, the thrill of a good bust.

GREENLIGHT

Chief looks like shit. He has dark, puffy half-moons under his eyes, and the creases in his forehead seem deeper than the last time I saw him. He must've gotten his ass chewed from somebody higher up about this. Inmates will always find a way to get drugs and other contraband into prisons, but there will always be somebody to blame for the oversight. Right now, I'm at the bottom, and I'm thankful Chief likes me and isn't taking it out on me too badly, other than the fact he's called me in on my day off to conduct the search. It sucks, but it could be worse.

"Have you had the water shut off to the cells yet?" I ask.

Corrections 101 for shakedowns: Shut the water off half an hour before a search. They will most likely flush the toilet and won't be able to flush again until the water comes back on. This makes it so they can't dispose of contraband when they see officers walk in.

I can tell by the look on his face he didn't. "No worries, I'll take care of it."

Ten minutes later, I stand at the front of the briefing room, looking at the five officers assigned to help me today. I recognize all but one; he must be new. I've not had much of a chance to get out and meet the latest class of officers out of the academy. I walk up and shake his hand. "I'm Lindsay Lanier with K-9. This here's Kody. I've not seen you around. Did you just graduate from the academy?"

"I'm CO Wright. I've been on the job for about three months now. I guess I've not been in the right place at the right time." He shoots me a wink with a smile. I'm sure he thinks he's charming, but I'm not impressed. I'm used to correctional officers hitting on me, and I'm not falling for it. I learned my lesson after my relationship with Ryan. The rumor mill here is worse than high school.

"Right," I say flatly and turn my attention to my team. "Okay, guys, we've been tasked with shaking down Baker Pod. I've called ahead and had the water shut off. They're still locked down from count, so they'll keep them that way until we get there. As we search each room, the inmates will be strip-searched and given a new uniform before they're sent out to the recreation field. The unit will let them back in once we've cleared the pod. I really need you guys to be thorough with your searches; we found a decent amount of meth on a female visitor yesterday, and we think it was supposed to go to this pod." Before I can continue with my briefing, I'm interrupted by CO Thompson. He's fat and lazy and one of the worst officers I've ever had the displeasure of working with.

"I'll do the logbook and the incident reports. I don't want to make the new guy look bad with my great shakedown skills."

"Don't you mean *fake*downs, Thompson?" Smith laughs. Smith's a good officer. He gets through his shift without any problems. Staff and inmates respect him, and he's generally good for a little comedic relief.

"Hey, man! That ain't right! I haven't seen you do any real searches in a long time." Thompson feigns offense, but he's laughing.

"Well, since I don't need any fakedowns," I say with a smile. "I think I will let you do the bitchwork, Thompson. Nobody else wants to do all the paperwork. Smith, I'm going to have you doing strip searches. Wright, you're going to help Smith with the strips and handing out the uniforms. Ochoa and Rogers, you're going to hit the cells with me."

Wright looks irritated with the task I assigned him, but he seems a little too eager to me, and I feel like he needs to be knocked down a peg or two and shown his place. What better way to do that than to make him look at a few dozen nuts and butts?

Rogers is the only other female on the crew today. I've worked with her a little in the past. She's a good officer, and I know she'll be a great asset digging around the cells. Ochoa is the same way. He's excellent, and I'm thrilled he's here.

Down in Baker, we pile into the sally port leading into the pod. The small triangular room feels cramped with all of us inside while we wait for the pod door to open. Kody pants heavily with excitement, subjecting us to his kibble breath.

I can see inmates' faces in the windows of their cell doors. A few disappear when they realize we're here to search. When the pod door pops, I hear a loud "Fuck!" echo off the cinder block walls of the empty day room. Somebody figured out they can't flush their toilet. This makes me laugh. I love when things go my way.

Kody and I walk the dayroom area of the pod. He's sniffing under the tables and around the phones, through the showers and the area with a sink and microwave. We check around the stairs, leading to the top tier and the porter's closet where they keep the mops and brooms with the watered-down cleaning chemicals. While we're making our rounds, the other officers are getting the pod set up. Wright's setting out uniforms, and Smith is searching the showers to make sure there isn't anything like razor blades left behind, since that's where he'll be performing strip-searches.

When we're all ready, I walk to the first cell on the bottom tier and call the control room on the radio to open the door. I hear the mechanical lock cycle and pull the door open. There's no need to tell the inmates what to do. They know the drill. The two residents from cell one walk out with their hands behind their backs, wearing nothing but a pair of prison-issue boxer shorts.

The cell is six feet wide by nine feet long. There are two metal bunks secured to the back wall over two narrow plexiglass windows. On the left-hand side, there's a small metal table with two small seats on each side, attached to the wall. The steel toilet-and-sink combo are at the front of the cell.

Kody and I make a sweep through the cell before getting out of the way so Ochoa and Rogers can comb through the inmates' possessions. Their storage boxes are filled with letters from family, their hygiene products, jewelry boxes and picture frames made from ramen noodle wrappers, and food they've bought from the commissary. Unfortunately, we also come across the occasional fi-fi; lonely nights lead to ingenuitive efforts for some mock feminine company.

With the first two inmates are dressed and sent to rec, I have the next room popped, and we continue through the pod. Fortunately, we've made it three quarters of the way through, finding nothing too major. Ochoa found a tattoo gun and some ink, and Rogers found a rusty shank in the sink of one room. When I investigated it, I discovered those two inmates are new. My guess is they didn't even know it was in there; a previous tenant probably left it behind, but these two will have to answer for it. Thankfully, I'm not the one to decide who takes the fall or what their consequences will be. I make sure Thompson documents everything correctly.

After Kody and I search the rooms on the bottom tier, we step back and let Ochoa and Rogers finish the last two rooms before we move to the top tier.

I notice something that shakes me. In the last cell on this tier, there is a picture on the wall of a truck, and it looks eerily similar to mine. The only difference is the rims. The truck in the picture has aftermarket wheels and tires, whereas mine are still stock. It could be a coincidence, but I can't ignore the knot in the pit of my stomach, like maybe there's more to it. Maybe I'm being arrogant to think it's about me, but I don't think so.

Butch Hammond is standing at his door in the far corner of the top tier, and he's staring daggers at me. His broad frame fills most of the long, narrow window. His shaved head, marred with scars, is only a few inches shy of the rivets holding the plexiglass in its frame. A thick salt-and-pepper goatee surrounds his thin lips. I'm sure he's already found out I'm the one who stopped his package from making it in through visitation, and now I'm here to find out if he's hiding anything in his house. I can practically see the smoke pouring out of his ears, but I stare right back at him for a few seconds. I won't let him intimidate me.

My first introduction to Butch was right after meeting Tenille. She invited me to go dancing at the bar with her on a night the entire ZMC was there celebrating a victory after a brawl with a smaller level street gang. She hadn't expected them to be there and warned me to keep my mouth shut about my new job. I felt like I had "CO" stamped in giant letters on my forehead. We hadn't been there more than five minutes before she was dragged away to dance with a man dressed in a black leather vest and jeans. I took a good look around and walked right back through the way I had come.

The next afternoon when she came to check on me, I made her tell me why she was hanging out with a biker gang. The man I watched her dance with was none other than Butch. He had been president of the club for the last fifteen years, after setting up the former president as a traitor and killing him in cold blood. He killed any member who opposed him. Once he took over, he turned the club, which had been mostly straight, into a criminal enterprise. They began manufacturing meth and running a prostitution ring to start. She didn't know the full extent of their criminal involvement.

He's been in prison on a petty possession charge for about a year, and as soon as he hit the yard, everybody fell in line. There's something about him that intimidates people into doing whatever he asks of them and then some. I've seen more than a few officers get fired from being compromised by him.

From the corner of my eye, I see Ochoa and Rogers coming out of the last room. I decide to break the staring contest with Hammond—and the tension—with a smile and wave before I turn away.

"What was that about?" Rogers asks as she grabs a bottle of water.

"Oh, nothing. Hammond's trying to intimidate me, and I wanted to show him it isn't working."

"Well, I think he got your message, and he's pissed about it. He punched his door before he walked away."

I shrug. "Well, I hope he hurt his hand. Let's start on that side and get him out of here. There's no reason to let him think we're scared to let him out of his room."

STEVIE LEE

When Hammond comes out, he's following procedure perfectly. His eyes lock on mine until he's forced to look away to walk down the stairs. When he passes me, in a low voice meant only for me to hear, he says, "Good luck, Lindsay."

The hairs on the back of my neck stand up. He knows my fucking first name. I know it's possible for these guys to find out information about us, but this feels malicious instead of a result of curiosity. I keep my face expressionless and lead Kody into the cell. It's pristine. They've made their beds perfectly, the room is devoid of trash, the floors are clean, and the stainless-steel sink and toilet are polished to a shine. You can tell this guy is the King Shit and has other inmates smuggling extra cleaning supplies in from the kitchen to clean his room for him.

Not that I expected to, but we found nothing in Hammond's cell. It's unlikely the leader of the prison's most notorious gang would keep contraband in his cell. He'd make someone much lower on the totem pole hide it for him.

I'm beginning to think we aren't going to find anything when Kody sits in the third-to-last cell on the tier. I call him up to sniff around again and he sits back down, staring at the vent above the sink. I casually walk out of the cell as officers lead the two inmates living here out the door. The second guy turns and looks at me with a worried look on his face. Once he's out of the sally port and into the hall, I shut the cell door behind me. I don't want it searched until all the inmates are out of the pod.

We get the last two rooms searched, and with the pod emptied of inmates, we go back into the room where Kody signaled. The vent looks like they've tampered with it. They recently scraped the paint off the screws.

Ochoa climbs on top of the toilet to get a better view and unscrews the vent cover easily by hand. He pulls out a peanut butter jar full of a white powdery substance. Within the powder, which appears to be sugar, is several baggies with little white crystals. Bingo.

I key the mic to my radio: "Lanier to Chief."

"Go ahead, Lanier."

"We've got it."

"Forty-five my office with it, now!"

"Copy that. Ten nineteen." I hate talking in ten codes, but they're necessary to keep radio traffic to a minimum. Forty-five basically means "come to/go to" and 10-19 is "in route."

I can't tell if Chief is happy or upset we found the drugs. I'm sure it's a mixture. He wants to be proud of his staff for finding contraband, but at the same time, he wants to be mad it made it into the facility in the first place. If they had found nothing, he'd be wondering if they'd done thorough searches. Neither scenario is ideal.

I pause in front of the ugly steel door leading to Chief's office. The many layers of paint are peeling and flaking. My stomach churns the more I think about the picture and Hammond saying my first name. I take a fortifying breath. I can't dwell on this. I have a job to do, and if I obsess over things that probably mean nothing, I'll never be able to walk through these gates without having a panic attack.

"I've already got the team writing their reports, and as soon as you sign a chain of custody form, I'll write up my report and be out of your hair to deal with this." I want to get these drugs out of my possession and get out of the line of fire as quickly as possible.

"All right, fine. Make sure they all write their reports well and turn them in as soon as possible. And tell those officers to keep their mouths shut about what you found today."

"Consider it done. I'll see you Monday, Chief." I'm almost through the door when Chief speaks.

"Lanier."

I stop and turn back to look at him.

"You did good today. Get some rest tonight, and get back here Monday

morning. I'm sure the warden is going to put you to work."
"Yes, sir."

CHAPTER 4

Monday morning, my phone chimes with a text message as soon as I park next to a familiar black truck. I check it quickly, knowing I only have five minutes to clear the walk-through scanner to get to the time clock.

Tenille: I just scored a pair of tickets to see Shawn Cross Friday night! Go with me!

Shawn is Tenille's favorite country singer. She's obsessed with his *Bro Country* brand of music. I prefer a more traditional sound, but I'm not an elitist. I'll listen to just about anything.

LL: Sounds fun. I'll see you Friday.

I make it to the time clock with thirty seconds to spare. As I'm swiping my badge, Chief appears from the administrative area where all the big wigs hide out.

"Lanier, Warden Pike wants to see you in his office." The color must drain from my face because he says, "Don't worry, you're not in trouble or anything. He really needs to talk to you about the ZMC drug thing."

I sigh with relief and make my way down the hall toward the administration offices. Inside the warden's office, I take the only available seat when Pike grimly gestures for me to sit. Warden Pike is a severe-looking man with a large forehead and long, sharp nose. His wavy brown hair slightly softens his features.

Chief said I wasn't in trouble, but I can't help feeling nervous, looking at the bleak expressions on the faces of the three men in the room. I know Warden Pike and the assistant warden, Keith Snyder, but the third man isn't someone I recognize. I'm not sure if he is causing the weakness in my knees or if it's the apprehension I feel being in this room.

He's gorgeous but in a rugged sort of way. Even though he's sitting, I can tell he's got to be over six feet tall and easily over two hundred pounds of solid muscle, clearly defined through his black T-shirt. His dark-brown hair is short on top and faded down to almost nonexistence on the sides. He doesn't look thrilled to be here, and his sheer presence intimidates me a little. I wonder who the hell he is and why he's here to begin with.

Warden Pike clears his throat and gets right down to business. "Lanier, late last night, an officer on graveyard intercepted a kyte from a fishing line. Butch Hammond has put a greenlight on your head."

I instantly feel the blood drain from my face, and beads of sweat collect across my forehead and upper lip. I swipe them away with a shaky hand. Pain wells in my chest as my heart thrashes wildly against my rib cage. To think I was proud of myself for disrupting their business… My pride is going to get me killed.

I take a few deep breaths to ease the tension in my throat and chest. I'm not going to let this rattle me. I'm strong. I straighten my spine, sitting up tall. They are not going to scare me into doing less than my best. I'm going to go back out there with my head held high and smile when I find their next package. They will not rattle me this easily.

"From the contents of the letter, it doesn't look like it was the only one sent, and we listened in on phone calls of known members of the Zona MC. From what we can tell, the threat has reached the streets as well."

This time, Snyder speaks up. He used to be my captain when I first started working at the prison, but he jumped the ranks and snagged a promotion to assistant warden about a year ago. Since then, I haven't talked to him a lot, but we used to be tight back in the day, even getting drinks together after our shift occasionally. Favoritism is huge, and I was lucky enough to be one of Snyder's favorites.

"Look, Linds, we aren't sure how serious this threat is, but we're not taking it lightly. Street value between these last two big busts is somewhere around ten grand. In here, it's probably worth triple or more. You've put a major hiccup in ZMC's drug operation, and I can't imagine Butch is going to take it lying down. This is Rhett Caraway. He and I were buddies back when we were in the corp."

I look at the hot guy sitting silently, who's barely given me more than a glance since I walked in. He's finally looking at me with an unreadable expression. "Rhett started his own private security company a few years ago and has agreed to take on this case as a favor to me. He's going to provide round-the-clock security for you until we know for sure you are safe."

The assumption I need a bodyguard is irritating, especially since it looks as though this guy doesn't even want to deal with me.

"So, what does that mean? He's going to sit outside of my house and follow me to work and shit? For how long? This seems ridiculous. Give me a gun locker, and I'll carry when I'm not here. I can protect myself. I don't need a bodyguard." I don't want anyone to perceive me as weak.

Rhett lets out a small snort and shakes his head. This irritates me further. He doesn't even know me, and he's laughing at me. What the fuck is his problem?

"Lanier, we're not taking any chances. The phone call was descriptive. Butch's second in command told somebody on the streets to run you off the road on your way home from work today. They gave a description of your truck and your address. They even had a surprisingly good idea of what time you should be leaving. They placed the call about forty-five minutes ago. We don't think there has been enough time for somebody to get down here to stake the place out, so we all think it would be best if Rhett takes you to a safe house immediately. He's going to pull his truck into the delivery area, and we're going to sneak you out of here in case they have somebody watching your truck in the parking lot. We figure we've got an eight-hour head start since they'll expect you to work all day. Before you go, there's something I'd like to show you. I think it will help you understand the gravity of the situation." Pike's tone is serious.

They turn the computer screen my way, and Pike clicks Play on a video. A young inmate I don't recognize is pacing the floor of a cramped holding room in the investigations department. He walks up to the camera in the corner of the room and speaks. Directly to me.

"Hey there, Lindsay bitch. Did you really think we'd sit back and let you interrupt my hustle without consequence? You'd better watch your back. We're coming for you, and we're going to make sure you earn the money we lost. That pretty little mouth and hot body of yours is going to come in handy when we offer you up to our clientele. You're going to wish we had enough mercy to just kill you." He growls before the video shuts off, and a different clip begins.

This time, Butch is sitting in a chair. Cuffs around his wrists connect to a belly chain, limiting his movements. A set of leg irons attached to the floor adorn his ankles. His slouched posture conveys his apathetic nature.

From a few feet away, Kennedy leans forward. His booming voice blares through the computer's speakers. "Mr. Hammond, we intercepted this kyte detailing a hit on Officer Lanier. You know anything about it?"

"What makes you think I'd know anything about it?" Butch asks nonchalantly.

"Come on now, don't be coy with me. Did you order your men to kill Officer Lanier?" Kennedy's voice is losing the casual tone he normally uses, his cool facade slipping into agitation.

A charismatic smile takes over Butch's face. "Does that really sound like something I would want to happen to the sweet Miss Lanier?" His eyes lift to the camera, and he winks.

The motherfucker *winks*. And who the hell was the first guy? He's an idiot. If Butch finds out he gave them up, he's deader than I am.

I sit quietly, contemplating what I've seen. All three men stare at me, waiting for my response. Worry etches Snyder's face. Rhett leans forward, his elbows braced on his knees.

"All right, I get it. Do I at least get to go home and pack some clothes, since it sounds like this is going to take a couple of days?"

"I think we've got enough of a head start we can swing by your place really quick. As long as we can get you out of here unnoticed and you pack quickly." This is the first time Rhett has said anything, and his voice is the sexiest thing I've ever heard.

I'm struck speechless. All I can muster is a slight nod.

"All right, I'll go pull my truck through the vehicle sally port." He shakes hands with Pike and Snyder and leaves the office.

I breathe out a held puff of air. I'm not sure how I'm going to survive in a safe house for a few days with that man. My attraction toward him is going to make the days long and the nights even longer. Snyder pulls me into a friendly hug and assures me everything will be okay, then he calls for the inmates in the halls to be secured so I can make my way to Rhett without being seen.

Five minutes later, I'm sitting in the front seat of the same sexy Dodge I saw, and it hits me. Rhett is the hot guy Tenille told me about the other day, when we had lunch. Good Lord, she wasn't lying. He's even hotter than any fantasy my mind could conjure up.

Why am I even worrying about this? I should be worried about getting kidnapped, raped, and murdered. And if I'm being honest, murder is the least of my worries out of those options.

How does this even work? I don't think a threat like this goes away in a week and I can go back to work like everything is fine. What's my endgame here? Do I have to move, find another job, and continue looking over my shoulder for the rest of my life?

What the fuck have I gotten myself into?

CHAPTER 5

Rhett drives straight to my house and follows me in so I can grab clothes and toiletries to get me through a few days. He sits on my bed and watches me as I move around my room.

A blush creeps up my cheeks as I imagine climbing on top of him and making good use of the bed. I shake my head and push the provocative images from my thoughts. From the drawer of my nightstand, I'm grabbing my gun and extra magazine when I accidentally bump the power button to my vibrator, and it buzzes to life. "Shit, shit, shit!" I drop my duffel bag on the floor and toss the gun and magazine in so I can shut the loud toy down.

I stand with my back toward Rhett, trying to pull myself together. I'm absolutely mortified, and his quiet laughter isn't making me feel better. I guess I should've listened to the lady at the dildo party when she said to store your toys without the batteries. It was kind of like a Tupperware party but for sex toys, and it's too late to heed her advice now, dammit. I take a deep breath and grab my bag from the floor. "I'm ready to go now," I mutter and head for the door.

"You sure you packed everything you need from your weapons drawer?" He's no longer holding back his laughter. He walks up behind me and puts his hand on the small of my back, leading me outside and to his truck. His touch does nothing to soothe my nerves.

He pulls open the passenger door for me and puts my bag in the back seat. Before I can close the door, he steps in the way and puts his hand on my knee. I force myself to look at him, knowing my face is probably still flushed. He looks like he wants to say something, but something holds him back.

I can't help but smile a little. His eyes convey so much emotion. I can see his sympathy plain as day.

Rhett closes my door. I watch him make his way around to his side of the truck. Goddamn, that man is sex on legs. Maybe I should've packed the extra weapon. Lord knows I'll be turned on constantly until I can get away from him. Who am I kidding? My fantasies of Rhett are going to run wild long after I return from captivity.

We ride along in silence for over an hour. Rhett has an oldies country radio station turned down low, and he quietly sings along occasionally. His voice is so sexy, he has me squirming in my seat. I'm a sucker for a man who can sing, even more so if he can play guitar.

I catch him glancing at me with a small smirk. I know he's thinking about my little mishap back in my bedroom.

Rhett's first to break the silence. "You know you've got nothing to be embarrassed about, right? It's no big deal."

"You're kidding, right? I basically announced to a stranger I keep my vibrator in the same drawer as my forty. Yeah, absolutely nothing to be embarrassed about." My words drip with sarcasm.

"We're going to be spending a lot of time together, and it's going to be really awkward if you can't let this go. Seriously, don't sweat it. I think it's hot when a woman takes control of her own needs."

"Oh my God." I bury my face in my hands as my skin heats again. "Can we please not talk about my masturbation habits or the things that turn you on? Jesus, you think our time together is going to be awkward by not talking about these things. I think this is worse!"

"Look, Lanier, I'm not trying to make this more awkward. We're stuck with each other for the foreseeable future, and we can't spend the entire time in silence. I'm trying to break the tension. If it bothers you that much, I won't bring it up again. Will you at least try to have a conversation with me? I can't stand sitting here in silence like this. We've got at least three more hours of driving, and I'm already going crazy in the quiet.

"I'm sorry for making this more awkward. I'm not used to anybody knowing something so personal about me, not to mention the fact you intimidate the shit out of me."

Rhett shoots me the most devastating smile I've ever seen, and the muscles tighten deep within my belly. "I intimidate you? You don't seem like the type of girl who intimidates easily. In fact, you kind of seem like a bit of a bad ass."

"I *don't* intimidate easily. It's why I'm so quiet. I feel completely out of my element. I feel like my whole life got turned upside down. I've walked into that prison every day for the last six years with my head held high. I've always had a healthy amount of fear, of course, but I've never felt rattled. Today, when Pike and Snyder told me about the threat, my first instinct was to blow it off. Inmates have threatened me a million times, but it's always bullshit. But I realized Snyder wouldn't be wasting your time for something petty, and I guess I've been a little off since then. And then the vibrator thing happened, and I don't know whether to laugh or cry."

I laugh, like hysterically laugh. I can't seem to stop; it's like all the tension that's built up over the last hour is finally breaking loose in the form of laughter. Apparently it is contagious because Rhett starts too.

"I'm glad you think this is funny." I smack him on the arm in mock indignation.

"I thought it was funny from the very beginning. Well, the vibrator thing, not the threat against you. That part isn't funny at all. You don't need to worry though. I'll keep you safe."

His words sober me instantly. I study his face for the first time. He looks at me and makes eye contact while we're stopped at a red light. His eyes are a vibrant shade of hazel with vivid touches of green. I can tell he's telling me the truth and I can trust him with my life.

The light turns green, and Rhett turns his gaze back to the road. I look around and realize I don't know where we are. We're on the outskirts of a small town I don't recognize. I've lived in this state my entire life and thought I knew it well, but right now, I'm at a complete loss. "I just realized I don't know where we're going."

Rhett runs his hand against his face. "Well, before you got yourself on the top of Butch Hammond's shit list, Keith was going to let me use his cabin up near Greer for the rest of the week to go fishing. It's why I was down there in that crappy prison town to begin with. I came down to get the keys from him and hang out for a few days before I headed north. When shit hit the fan, he asked me to bring you along, knowing there was no way anybody would find you, and protect you until it's safe for you to go back to work. We're taking the scenic route to make sure we aren't being followed."

"This ugly little town doesn't seem so scenic. Any idea how long it's going to take to get this all resolved?"

"Tired of me already?" he asks with a grin. "No idea, sugar. I've never dealt with anything like this before. My company doesn't handle this type of detail. We provide the security at the concert pavilion."

"Not tired of you, but I'm a little concerned about your qualifications now. The ZMC is probably a little more dangerous than some drunken asshole trying to grab Taylor Swift's ass. Anyway, I'm sure you're more than a little irritated to be having to take care of me instead of some cute celebrity."

"I'll be honest. I was pretty pissed you were crashing my fishing trip, but when I finally quit sulking and actually looked at you… I wasn't so upset anymore." He shoots me a panty-dropping smile. "And there's no need to worry about my qualifications. Three tours in Iraq leave me more than qualified to take on a couple of ex-cons."

I don't know what to say in return, so I watch the scenery out the window.

After several awkward moments of silence, Rhett pipes up again. "I wanted to ask back there, but it didn't feel like the right time. What the heck is a kyte?"

"It's what inmates call a letter. Or sometimes it can be a request to their counselor."

"And a fishing line? How does that work?" he asks with genuine curiosity.

I forget the things that seem so mundane to me about prison life are fascinating to people who haven't been around it. "They make a line out of strips of bedsheets tied together, or they make a string out of trash bags wound tightly. They weigh it down with something. I see a tube of toothpaste most often, and then they toss it from beneath their cell door. Another inmate will toss his line out and snag the first, pulling it into his cell to retrieve whatever it is they're passing," I explain.

"Why don't they wait until they're not in their cells? Don't they get time to wander around or something?"

"In a normal housing unit, yeah. But if they're on lockdown or in segregation, they don't get that luxury. It's actually pretty funny to watch. Things can get boring when you're working a lockdown pod. We had an officer who would entertain himself by putting an extra sack lunch at the front of the pod just to watch them 'fish' for it all day."

He glances at me with a smirk. "So it's not like it is on TV with fights breaking out all the time?"

"Nah." I shake my head. "I mean, shit happens, but not as often as you'd think. Corrections is honestly quite monotonous."

His smirk turns sad. "I bet you're wishing it was boring right now."

Ain't that the truth.

I must've fallen asleep because the next thing I know, Rhett is shaking my shoulder. "Lanier. Wake up, sugar. We're here."

I rub the sleep from my eyes and stretch my arms. "You can call me Lindsay, you know."

Rhett smiles and jumps out of his truck.

After we get the truck unloaded, I walk around the small cabin in search of the bathroom. I find the only bathroom connected to the only bedroom containing the only bed. I walk back out to the living room to see if the sofa is large enough to sleep on. It's not. It's a small love seat even I couldn't lie on comfortably.

It looks like Rhett and I are going to have to share the full-size bed. He must see the concern in my eyes as he walks in from unloading an ice chest of food into the refrigerator.

"What's wrong? Cabin not up to your standards?"

"No, that's not it at all. It's nice. I'm used to camping in tents. I'm excited to have plumbing."

"Then what's the matter? I can tell you're bothered by something."

"Um, I noticed there is only one bed."

"Don't worry, Lindsay. I'll sleep on the couch."

I raise my eyebrows, and we both turn to look at the tiny love seat.

"Or in the bed of my truck," he says.

"You can't do that! It's going to get cold at night up here. Look, I can stay on my side of the bed if you can do the same. We have no idea how long we're going to be up here, so we might as well try to be as comfortable as we can."

"If you're sure…"

I nod.

"Okay, I appreciate that. I wasn't looking forward to freezing my balls off in the hard bed of my truck, but I would've done it to make you feel better."

"Well, I'd hate for your balls to freeze off." The words are out of my mouth before I can stop them, and my face goes warm again.

Rhett laughs. "Good to know you're concerned about my balls. Maybe later—" His cell phone rings in his pocket. He glances at the screen and walks toward the kitchen before he answers it.

I can only hear bits and pieces of what he's saying, but I'm willing to bet he's talking to Snyder. I can tell he's updating him on our little road trip. Not knowing what to do with myself and feeling a little awkward about the way our conversation was going, I decide to take a little walk around outside and scout the area. I'm hoping the fresh air will clear my head, and I can use some distance from Rhett to ease the sexual tension quickly building between us.

I've got to get a handle on this before things get away from me. I'm not the type of girl to jump in bed with some guy. Not to mention sleeping with Rhett would further complicate my already-complicated situation. They hired him to protect me, not fuck me. I need to focus on what I'm going to do after Butch's threat goes away… if it's ever resolved.

I realize there may not be a resolution. The greenlight is already out, and there's no way of knowing how many people know about it. I know they can segregate the ones within the prison and control their communication to a point, but Pike said they'd already placed a call to the outside, so somebody on the streets is looking for me. There's really no way to completely control how far this threat reaches. I may never return to work.

I sit under a tall ponderosa pine tree overlooking a meadow, and I draw in a lungful of clean mountain air. I feel myself relax marginally. I don't have to come up with all the answers right now. I'm sure I'll be up here for a few days with nothing else to do.

Unfortunately, I can't shake my feelings of desperation, and a few tears slide down my cheeks. How fucking pathetic. I never cry, and I can't believe I'm crying now. I wipe my tears away and steal another deep breath.

"Lindsay!" The screen door to the cabin slams, and I realize Rhett must be worried about me wandering off.

I call out to him from about fifty yards away, and he jogs toward me. "Sorry about that, sugar. You didn't have to hide out here. That was Keith. He wanted to check up on us and see how you were doing. He was curious if there was anybody we needed to call and let them know you were okay. Like a boyfriend or something..." He's got to be fishing for that last bit of information.

"Oh, shit." I groan. "I totally forgot I have plans to go to a concert with my friend Tenille this weekend."

"Oh. Um, do you have your friend's phone number? I can have Keith call her for you," he says sympathetically.

"Can't I use your phone to call her? I have a bad track record of breaking plans with her and would rather be the one to give her the news."

"I'm not supposed to let you call anybody, but I can have Keith call Tenille for you. Maybe it's better if he tells her; then she'll know you aren't bailing because you want to."

"No, it's not a good idea. I don't think Snyder would approve of me being best friends with an associate of the Zona MC. Are you sure I can't call her from your phone?"

"We don't want this phone number to be traced to anybody close to you. They can track my phone through the GPS. I'm sorry."

"It's fine. When I'm not home, she'll probably drive by and see my truck still at the facility and think I got stuck at work. Then tomorrow she'll probably think I'm blowing her off. She'll be heartbroken, but she always forgives me, eventually."

"What about you?"

I give him a confused look.

"Are you heartbroken?"

"I don't know if heartbroken is the right word. Scared and confused seem to be more accurate," I say glumly.

He offers me a sad smile. "Come on, sugar, let's take a walk down to the water. You look like you could use some cheering up." He reaches down to take my hand and helps me stand. When I'm on my feet, I expect him to drop my hand, but he doesn't. He laces our fingers together and walks farther into the tree line.

I wonder what his intentions are. Is he trying to show some affection by holding my hand—which seems completely unprofessional—or does he think I'm some fragile female who needs the comfort?

We spend about an hour down at the lake. It was only about a ten-minute hike from the cabin. We take off our shoes, roll up our pants, and wade around in the freezing-cold water. I challenge him to a rock-skipping contest, and he kicks my ass. I haven't had this much fun in a long time.

We joke and talk shit to each other like old friends. After Rhett saves me from almost falling on my ass in the water, he suggests we give it up for the day and head back to the cabin to make dinner.

After eating, I take a shower and change into a pair of leggings and a baggy T-shirt to sleep in. In our rush to get on the road, I didn't bother changing out of my uniform, so it feels wonderful to be in something more comfortable. My scalp aches from being pulled back so tightly all day. I nose around the bathroom, looking for some pain killers with no luck.

When I walk back into the living room, Rhett is slouching on the love seat in nothing but a pair of lounge pants that sit low on his hips. He looks like he was ripped from the pages of a fitness magazine.

My gaze drifts across his chest and down his washboard abs. I can't help but lick my lips and drag my bottom lip between my teeth at the sight of the well-defined "v" disappearing into his waistband. I'm pulled back to reality when Rhett clears his throat. I snap my eyes back up toward his face, embarrassed he caught me so blatantly staring at his body.

"Enjoying the view?"

I should've known he'd never let me get away with it. He seems to enjoy my embarrassment way too much, but his cocky grin makes me weak in the knees. I close my eyes for a second and try to regain my wits. The ache in my scalp throbs and brings me back to reality.

"Do you have any ibuprofen or something? I've got a bit of a headache." I ask, completely ignoring his question.

"No, sorry. There might be some in the bathroom."

"There isn't. I checked. Maybe I'll go lie down. It's kind of been a long day, anyway." I turn to walk back into the bedroom, but Rhett reaches out and grabs my hand, stopping me in my tracks. He turns so his back is against the armrest and his leg runs along the back of the couch. He pulls me down to sit in front of him, sinks his long fingers into my hair, and massages my scalp. It feels so good, I can't help the small moan escaping my lips. He pulls me back softly to where I'm flush against his chest to continue working his magic. I settle in and close my eyes, giving in to the relief his touch provides.

"Feeling any better?" He's stopped rubbing my scalp and has laid my head on his shoulder, resting his cheek against my temple. He kneads down my arms, from my shoulders to my hands, where he laces our fingers together again and rests them on my stomach.

I relax into him and turn my face slightly toward his. It feels like heaven wrapped in his strong arms. He presses a small kiss to the corner of my eye, and I feel something stir to life at the small of my back. That's when I realize what's happening, and I have no idea what to do. This is so inappropriate. He's been hired to protect me, not seduce me, which he is well on his way to doing. I've completely let down my guard.

"Um, much better, thanks." I sit up but can't bring myself to look at him. "Well, I'm kind of tired, so I think I'm going to go to bed now." I get up and head toward the bedroom. I pull my gun from my duffle bag and rack a round into the chamber before setting it on the nightstand. At least I'll be prepared if some psycho finds me. I'm not so sure I'm as prepared to handle Rhett.

When I turn to crawl into bed, I notice him standing in the doorway, watching me. He looks nervous.

"Hey, Lindsay, we good?"

"Yeah, of course."

I'm a little nervous about sharing the bed with him now. There's no denying our attraction to one another, and I'm not sure I trust myself. It's only the first night and we're already struggling to behave. I settle into bed with my back toward the middle, trying to stay as close to the edge as I can without falling off. I'm afraid I'll lose my resolve and give in to temptation if I touch him at all. Rhett doesn't seem as concerned with keeping away from me and lies on his back. "Good night, Rhett."

"Night, sugar."

CHAPTER 6

Early the next morning, I gasp awake from a delicious dream about Rhett, further evidenced by the intense spasms between my legs. Holy shit, I've had a wet dream with the object of my desires lying next to me.

I slowly turn my head toward his side of the bed, hoping he's still sleeping, and find he's not there at all. I rub my hands against my face, relieved he didn't catch me in my moment of vulnerability. When I look up, I see Rhett standing in the bathroom doorway with a towel slung low around his hips. He's watching me with a shit-eating grin on his face. Son of a bitch. So much for not getting caught.

"Did you just have a sex dream?"

This man can't ever seem to let things go. He has a habit of calling me out too, making an embarrassing situation mortifying.

"I heard you moaning and thought something might be wrong. I came out here to see you writhing and arching your back," he says with a barely contained laugh.

I close my eyes, trying to regain my composure. Enough is enough, I decide. I'm not going to let him get to me anymore. We'll be cooped up in this little cabin together for several days, and I'll be damned if I'm going to let him constantly embarrass me.

With renewed confidence, I climb out of bed, push past him into the bathroom, and close the door. Rhett quietly calls my name with obvious worry. My answer is the sharp click of the lock sliding into place.

The bathroom is muggy with the steam from Rhett's shower. I slide the window open a crack to let in some fresh air so I can breathe. I hear his bare feet pad into the bedroom, giving me the privacy I so need right now.

After using the toilet, I brush my teeth and splash cold water on my face to extinguish what's left of the flush on my cheeks. Feeling better, I decide to get dressed and take a walk back down to the water to do some thinking and try to get a little more perspective on how to make my time with Rhett easier. I've got to get a handle on my attraction for him and find a way to deal with his obvious attraction for me. Maybe when this is over, we can see where things go, but for now, it's best if we keep our hands to ourselves. I take a deep breath and head back into the bedroom to retrieve my clothes.

Rhett is sitting on the bed, still wearing the towel. Before I can turn away from him, he stalks toward me, takes my face in his hands, and crushes his lips to mine. I lose my balance from the force of his kiss, which causes me to brace my hands against the solid expanse of his chest. My fingers inadvertently graze one of his nipples, and he lets out a deep groan. The sound of it weakens my knees and causes my panties to dampen. Rhett wraps his arms around my back. One hand cradles my head and the other grips my ass as he deepens our kiss. I give myself over to him, unable to fight the attraction any longer.

He slides his hands down and grips the back of my legs as I'm lifted off the floor and wrap them around his waist. His towel comes untucked and falls to the floor. His freed erection rubs against my core, causing a moan of my own to escape.

Rhett carries me to the bed and lays me down. Kneeling above me, he pulls my shirt over my head, then tugs my leggings and panties down in one swift motion. It gives me the opportunity to appreciate his powerful body and large cock standing proudly between his legs. I drag my bottom lip between my teeth as my eyes travel back up his body toward his face.

He climbs back on top of me and kisses me again. His hands knead my breasts and pinch my nipples, bringing them to attention. He kisses down my neck to my chest, where he swirls his tongue around each of my nipples before continuing down my stomach.

I gasp and arch my back off the bed when his tongue finds my clit. He glides two fingers into my pussy and curves them up toward my G-spot. "Goddamn, Lindsay, you're so wet." He continues to stroke my G-spot while licking and sucking my clit. It doesn't take long before my legs are quivering in anticipation of the building orgasm.

"Oh, fuck! Rhett." I gasp as an orgasm tears through me. Before I can come down from my high, Rhett slides into me. When he's fully inside, he pauses and presses a soft kiss to my lips.

"Is this okay, baby?"

I nod and raise my hips, encouraging him to move. It's been a long time since I've been with a man, and Rhett is by far the largest. His girth is stretching me and causing a slight burn, but the pleasure far outweighs the pain. I meet him thrust for thrust, his pelvic bone brushing against my clit. It doesn't take long before I'm teetering on the edge of another orgasm.

"Rhett, I'm going to come," I whisper into his ear. Gripping his shoulders, I pull myself up closer to him, and my head falls back in ecstasy. Rhett sinks his teeth into the flesh where my neck meets my shoulder, and he growls as he comes deep within me.

When our breathing finally returns to normal, he pulls out of me and rolls onto the bed beside me. He pulls me onto his chest and kisses the top of my head. We lie like that for a long time as I listen to his heartbeat.

Suddenly, he stiffens beneath me. "Shit, Lindsay? Are you on birth control?"

My heart stops, and my eyes go wide. I sit up and look into his worried expression, and I feel his semen leak from between my legs.

GREENLIGHT

The sensation overwhelming me is a strong reminder of the mistake we made. I snatch the towel from the floor and shove it between my legs as I run for the bathroom. I turn on the shower and wait for it to warm.

My mind is frantically running through possible scenarios and trying to calculate where I'm at in my cycle. I decide the odds of getting pregnant are slim, and if it happens, there's nothing we can do about it now anyway. I have enough to worry about with the threat against my life. I'm going to take things as they come. There's no use in worrying myself sick over a pregnancy that might not even come to be, and there's no way I'm going to regret what Rhett and I did. It was too amazing.

Rhett walks in as I climb into the shower to wash away the sticky evidence of our lovemaking.

"Lindsay, I'm sorry. I was so caught up in the moment, I didn't stop to think about whether you were on birth control, and I don't have any condoms up here. I shouldn't have touched you. I'm really sorry."

The look on his face breaks my heart. I can't let him take all the blame for this. I knew I wasn't on birth control and didn't stop to ask about a condom, so I'm as much to blame, if not more, for our little slipup.

I grab his hand and pull him into the shower with me. I go up on my tippy toes to brush a soft kiss to his lips and look into his eyes. "Rhett, this is as much my fault. Don't beat yourself up. Nothing may come of this. Let's not worry about it until there's something to worry about."

His relief is clear. I playfully poke my finger into his chest and try my best to look stern. "We can't continue to be so careless. We're going to have to behave ourselves until this is all over."

"Just so you know, if you end up pregnant, I'll take care of you and the baby. I won't abandon you or anything. We're going to have to sort out protection. After what happened between us, there is no way in hell I'm going to be able to keep my hands to myself. My hand will never be enough after being inside of you."

I can't help but laugh. Rhett pulls me close and kisses me deeply. My body heats with arousal.

"After we're done here, I'll call Keith and see if there's any news. Maybe it's safe enough to run into town this morning and grab breakfast, and while we're there, we can pick up the necessary provisions."

We continue to kiss and explore each other's bodies. We may not be able to have sex again, but that won't stop me from getting to know Rhett a little more intimately. I kiss my way down his chest and lick the water from his muscles. After dropping to my knees, I run my hand up and down the length of his cock. I lick the drop of moisture that's gathered at the tip before drawing him into my mouth. He groans loudly and cradles the back of my head as he leans back against the shower wall. I love seeing his reaction. There's something so sexy about knowing I'm the one making him lose control.

While Rhett calls Keith, I sit beneath the pine tree at the edge of the meadow and soak in the sun. I remind myself not to get my hopes up for a relationship with Rhett. When this whole thing blows over and we go back home, he'll probably forget about me. Hell, we don't even live in the same town. I'm not sure I can make a normal relationship work with my work schedule, let alone a long-distance one.

He was so sweet this morning when he reassured me he'd stick by me if I end up pregnant. And he's so fucking hot. He's got a great sense of humor, even though it's been mostly at my expense. He seems so perfect; I could see myself falling for him easily. I've got to remain objective and take our time together for what it is: an opportunity to have great fantasy sex with a man who could grace the cover of a romance novel.

The sound of Rhett's boots crunching against pine needles and decomposed granite pulls me from my thoughts. He kneels beside me and pulls my face toward him for a kiss. When he breaks away, he studies my face as if he's looking for something specific in my expression. "You okay, baby?"

"Yeah, I'm great. Just doing some thinking. The last twenty-four hours have been a lot to take in. What did Keith have to say?"

"They arrested a man who snuck into the parking lot of the prison last night trying to mess with your truck. They've been interrogating him ever since, trying to get some information on how far Hammond is going to take this threat. We're probably safe to make a quick trip into town, but we'll probably be staying up here for a few more days. It sounds like we completely fooled them with our quick escape," he says with an arrogant smile.

CHAPTER 7

Rhett pulls into a gas station and to a diesel pump to fill up his truck. Before jumping out, he reaches over and takes my hand, drawing my attention to him. "I'm going to set up the pump, then head inside to get what we need. Do you need me to get you anything else?"

I shake my head, and he hops out of the truck.

Rhett is still inside the store when I hear the pump shut off, so I jump out to take care of it. I top off the tank, stopping when the dollar amount rounds off evenly, and replace the nozzle in the cradle. After twisting the cap into place and closing the fuel door, I turn to get back into the truck but walk right into the solid expanse of Rhett's chest. I smile at him and push onto my tippy toes to kiss his cheek. He wraps an arm around my waist and holds me in place. The affection between us is easy and natural. I can't get enough.

"You didn't have to do all that." He gestures at the pump. "I would've taken care of it when I got here."

"I know, but there isn't any reason I shouldn't help where I can. I'm not some helpless female."

"I don't think you're helpless. I feel weird letting you fuel up my truck."

"Technically, you didn't let me. I just did it, so don't beat yourself up about it." I lean upward and whisper in his ear, "I'm sure you'll make it up to me later." I drag his earlobe between my teeth and place a soft kiss to the pulse on his throat. Then I push away from him and climb back into the truck. When I reach out to close my door, he's still standing there, staring at me. "Hurry up, let's go! I'm hungry!" It's nice to be the one leaving him speechless for a change.

We sit and have breakfast at a small diner. Rhett's telling me about his company and his employees. He's got a large crew of men and women who run security for him and his little sister, Kelly, who helps to manage the administrative side. He tries to stay behind the scenes as much as possible, but depending on staffing, he sometimes works the concerts as well.

"Don't celebrities usually travel with their own security?"

"Yeah, they do. My team covers the whole venue, not necessarily the artists themselves. There are only a few guys allowed to cover the backstage areas. They request me to cover that detail quite a bit since my cousin, Shawn, has gained some fame. He's dropped my name to other artists on his label."

"Wait a minute; your cousin is Shawn Cross?"

Before he can answer, we're interrupted by somebody calling my name. My eyes go wide with fear. Nobody up here should know me. I frantically look around the diner until I lock eyes with a guy walking up to our table.

I recognize him. He's an officer at one of the other prisons, whom I met while running K-9 through their facility as a favor last year. This guy followed me around the two days I was there, begging me to go out with him. No matter how many times I told him I don't date correctional officers, he wouldn't take the hint. He tried to convince me he was better than the other men who chose our profession and he needed the chance to prove himself to me.

I didn't have the heart to tell him his job wasn't the only turnoff. The fact he was at least twenty years older than me and three inches shorter had been factors as well. And now he's standing by our table, beaming down at me.

"Lanier! I thought that was you! It's so great to see you!" He leans down and wraps me in a hug like we're old friends. I'm trying to remember the dude's name, but it's not coming to me. I don't know what to do. I know I've got to get the guy to go away and quit drawing attention to us, but I've also got to figure out a way to keep him from telling anybody he's seen me.

"Oh, hi. What are you doing way out here?" I ask him, to buy myself time to come up with something reasonable to say.

"I come up here to visit my brother as often as I can. He works for the forest service. Here, let's take a selfie and I'll post it to Facebook. The guys are never going to believe I ran into you." He's already pulling out his cell phone to snap a picture, and I look to Rhett for help, my eyes bugging out. There is no way he can post my picture and location to social media. I'll be dead tonight if he does.

As if sensing my panic, Rhett gently pushes the guy's hand down. "Hey, man. Do you mind not taking a picture with my girlfriend? She had to call in sick to come up here with me, and I'd hate for her to get in trouble if her supervisors see her splashed across Facebook."

I could fucking kiss him right now. It made perfect sense and was completely believable.

The creeper startles and looks at Rhett like he hadn't noticed him before.

"Oh, shit. I'm sorry, I didn't even think about it. No problem, I'll go sit back down. It was really good to see you, Lanier." I can tell he's disappointed we ruined his opportunity for a selfie. I forgot this guy was the king of selfies. He's constantly posting pictures of himself with his dog. I mean, I post pictures all the time of me and Kody, but this is where gender bias works in my favor. I made the right decision in not going out with him.

"Good to see you too. Do you mind not telling anybody you saw me? My supervisor was really pissed I called in, so if he were to find out I wasn't really sick, I'd be in a lot of trouble." I give him my best smile, hoping to charm him into silence.

"Sure, you got it. See you later." He gives me a sad smile and a wave as he walks back to his table.

Rhett quickly pays the check, and we get back into his truck to head for the cabin. A few miles down the road, he asks, "You going to tell me what that was all about?"

I groan and rub my forehead. I tell him about the creeper's stalking and how his social media habits mimic those of a twelve-year-old girl. Rhett glances at me with raised eyebrows and laughs.

"You mean that little short guy thought he had a chance with you? He's old enough to be your dad!"

"Actually, I think he has a son my age. He really thinks he has game though. I got a message from him a few months ago asking me to meet him before work for 'a big hug.' I told him I was allergic to hugs, and I haven't heard from him again until today. As you can see, he doesn't take a hint, and he's not easily deterred."

Rhett reaches over and rubs my thigh. "So, Lanier, you think I could get a 'big hug' later?"

I punch his shoulder. "You're an asshole! Just for that, I don't think I'm going to give you any more big hugs. I guess you wasted your money on these condoms." I throw the box across the console and into his lap.

"Hey, now! I'm just teasing you. You were in a complete panic back there; I wanted to lighten things up a bit. Make you laugh. I don't think I've ever seen you so tense, not even when Keith told you you were on a hit list. Somebody wants to kill you, and you act like it's no big thing. Some old guy wants to take a selfie with you, and you about shit a brick. You can't hold out on me for one little joke." He's pouting at me, trying to be cute. It's working. A little too well.

"You've never seen me so tense? We've known each other all of twenty-four hours. And I panicked about the selfie because of the threat. Well, and a little bit because I don't want to be associated with that creep! Oh, and by the way, what was with calling me your girlfriend? That seemed a little unnecessary."

I stare at him across the truck, waiting for his response. He glances at me and shrugs. "I don't know. Wishful thinking, I guess."

Once again, I'm speechless. This never happens. I've got to have the last word and can usually come up with a witty comeback, but for whatever reason, Rhett leaves me with nothing to say. I'll admit, the idea of being with Rhett is rather appealing. Maybe I need to quit overthinking this whole situation and let it happen.

There are so many unknowns within my life right now I might as well add a relationship with Rhett to the list. I suddenly feel like I need some time to myself to just breathe. I'm used to coming home to an empty house where I can decompress and relax, but I've been stuck in the close confines of this truck or the cabin with Rhett for the last day and a half. It doesn't help that bouncing along this dirt road has the seam of my jeans creating perfect friction against my clit with every rut and pothole. My mind is a little muddled.

As we pull up to the gate leading to the cabin, I make a hasty decision to walk the rest of the way. I snatch the key for the lock from the cup holder and jump out of the truck before Rhett can even get into neutral. As he pulls through the gate, he yells through the window, saying I didn't have to get the gate. I ignore him and secure the lock back into place.

Instead of getting into the truck, I walk to the driver's side window and hand the key to him. "I'm going to walk the rest of the way."

"Lindsay, get back in the truck."

I shake my head at him and turn to walk away.

He drives slowly beside me, trying to get me to talk to him. "Are you mad I was teasing you about that guy? I'm sorry; I'll try to tone it down a bit.

I know I've been picking on you a lot."

"Rhett, just go. I'm not mad at you. I need some time to myself. It's only about a half-mile walk. I'll be there in fifteen minutes." I smile at him, trying to set him at ease. It must work because he nods and drives off.

I walk slowly, wanting to drag out my time alone as long as I can. I know when I get back to the cabin, we're going to have to talk. I'm thinking more clearly now that there's a little distance between us. The cloud of lust fogging up my brain has lifted somewhat.

If I'm being realistic, I have no future with Rhett. Once this is all over, he's going to go back to his life and his company and forget all about me, and I'm going to be heartbroken. He's the first guy I've had any interest in since Ryan, which was almost four years ago. I can already feel myself getting in over my head. I shouldn't have slept with Rhett this morning. And the way we behaved afterward, all lovey-dovey like we were together… God, what was I thinking?

I wasn't thinking. That's the problem. I let my body take over. His kisses are amazing, and I can't help but lose myself in his hazel eyes. I won't even get started on his body… Good Lord, the man is fine, but he's sweet and funny too. He's somebody I can see myself falling for under different circumstances. Who am I kidding? I'm falling for him under the current circumstances.

With the cabin in view, I make up my mind. I'm going to talk to Rhett and tell him I can't have sex with him again. I've got to protect myself, and I know I won't come out of this unscathed if I don't stop this now.

It sounds like he's chopping wood out back, so I round the corner and come to an abrupt stop at the sight of his naked back as he powerfully swings an ax over his head and sinks it into a piece of wood balanced on a stump. He bends to pick up the fallen pieces of split wood, and his jeans pull tight across his firm ass, and all thoughts of not having sex with him slip from my mind.

I lean against the cabin to watch him in lumberjack mode when I knock over a shovel I hadn't noticed propped against the wall. He whips around to face me at the sound of the crash.

"You're back. How was your walk?" His face shows some apprehension. I guess he didn't believe me when I said I wasn't mad.

My gaze drags from his face to his beautifully sculpted chest and abs. When I reach his zipper, I blush at the memory of our shower this morning. I look back up at his face and realize he's smirking. He's probably remembering the same thing.

I step forward and lay my hand on his chest, over his heart. My fingers itch to trace the tight muscles, but instead, I reach up and run my fingers along the stubble of his jawline.

He waits for me to make another move. His breathing is a little labored from chopping the wood, but it's slowly evening out, and he relaxes into my touch. All thoughts of protecting myself disappear. I'm going to get hurt—I know it—but I can't seem to help myself. I lean up and gently kiss his lips. Rhett grabs my hips with both hands and pulls my body in closer, deepening the kiss. I'm giving myself emotional whiplash.

His fucking phone rings, completely breaking the spell we've fallen under. I step back, giving him a chance to retrieve it from the pocket of his pants.

"Hey, man, what's up?" He gives me a small apologetic smile while he listens to whoever is on the other line. I feel like I should give him some privacy, so I point at the cabin and turn to walk inside. Before I can get two steps away, Rhett grabs my arm, pulls me against his side, and presses a quick kiss to the top of my head.

I wrap one arm around his lower back and rub my other hand along his abs. I'm lost to my exploration. When my hands graze the waistband of his jeans and my fingers creep beneath it, his breath catches, and he grabs my hand, halting my progress. This makes me smile. It's nice to know I'm not the only one affected.

GREENLIGHT

Rhett clears his throat, bringing my attention back to his face. He's playfully glaring at me and shaking his head. "Email me your flight information, and I'll be there to pick you up Thursday." He pauses for a second while he listens.

I wiggle my fingers beneath his hand, trying to inch my way into the front of his pants.

"Hey, brother, I've got to go, but I'll see you on Thursday." He pushes his phone into his back pocket and picks me up, then slams me against the cabin.

His mouth crashes against mine in a bruising kiss. With one arm wrapped underneath my ass, he snakes the other up my back, grabs a handful of hair, and jerks my head back to give him unhindered access to my neck. I drag my nails across his broad shoulders, eliciting a moan from deep in Rhett's chest.

In a move I can only describe as pure talent, Rhett pulls my boot from my left foot and works my pant leg and panties down. He switches arms beneath my ass, then frees my other leg from my pants, baring me from the waist down while holding me suspended from the ground. I'm damn impressed and ridiculously turned on.

Rhett has a smug smile on his face. Apparently, he's impressed with himself as well and, judging by the solid bulge in the front of his jeans, just as turned-on. I reach between us, unbuckle his belt, and tear his jeans open. With his hard cock freed, I line him up with my opening and he thrusts deep, filling me completely. He pauses to kiss me and give me a chance to adjust to his size. Gripping my shoulder, he begins a hard, punishing rhythm. With every forward thrust, he slams my body down on him. Every time our bodies connect, a jolt of electricity surges through me, building toward an intense orgasm.

"Come for me, baby. I can't hold out much longer." Rhett's muscles quiver under my fingertips, and the look of pure lust in his eyes is enough to send me over the edge into pure bliss. The moment I fall, the sky opens, and a slow rain begins. Before I can come down from my high, Rhett finds his release. He drops his forehead to my shoulder, panting hard as a shudder runs through his entire body. "Jesus Christ, Lindsay. I've never come so hard in my life."

Those are my thoughts exactly. Sometimes a girl just needs to get fucked. The cold water dripping from the roof of the cabin drips onto my face, bringing me out of my lust-induced haze. "Maybe we should go in out of the rain."

Without another word, Rhett carries me into the cabin before withdrawing from me and setting me on my feet. That's when I notice his frown.

"What's the matter?"

"We slipped up again. I'm sorry. I don't know why I don't have any control when it comes to you. I've never been so careless with sex. What are the odds I've knocked you up?"

To say his question catches me off guard is an understatement. I never thought I'd be having a conversation like this with a man I hardly know, two minutes after having the best sex of my life. As Rhett tucks himself back into his pants and does up his belt, I realize I'm still standing here awkwardly, naked from the waist down. I tug the hem of my T-shirt down, trying to regain a little modesty.

"I'm going to go clean up and put some clothes on. Would you mind getting my jeans and boots from outside before the rain completely ruins them?" I can't hide the slight irritation in my voice at his callous question. The euphoria from moments ago is gone.

When I step from the shower a few minutes later, Rhett is leaning against the doorframe of the bathroom, watching me with apprehension. I can tell he's worried about my reaction, and my anger fades a little. When he looks at me with a little sadness in his eyes, my resolve disappears. It's like trying to discipline a little kid whose cuteness makes you smile and ruins any chance you have of following through.

    I decide not to acknowledge him until I'm fully dressed. I don't want to have this conversation while I'm naked and he's not. I don't like the dynamic it creates, like he's somehow more in control than I am. I won't let him make me feel vulnerable, even if it's only my perception and not truly his intention.

    Once I'm dressed, I make my way to the kitchen to grab a beer from the fridge. I feel like this is going to get heavy, and I could use a little buzz. As my fingers wrap around the cool glass bottle, I realize we're about to consider the possibility of me being pregnant and I'm trying to drink. I reluctantly leave the beer and swipe a bottle of water instead. I offer one to Rhett, who's followed surreptitiously behind me.

    "No, thanks. I'll take a beer though."

    The bastard, of course he will. I roll my eyes and hand it to him, then sit at the small table in the kitchen. I feel safer with the table between us instead of right next to him on the tiny couch. I might keep my wits about me with a barrier.

    Rhett sits across from me and twists the top off his beer. His eyes never leave mine as he takes a long pull. I watch the way his throat moves as he swallows. I never realized how sexy it was until this moment. I press my thighs together, trying to dull the ache stirring between them. Damn him.

    I've never reacted to a man like I do with him. I don't know what it is about him that has my mind scrambled to where I can't seem to be rational or reasonable. I won't even mention the way my body goes out of control with nothing more than a smile sent my way.

    He finally puts me out of my misery and takes the lead.

    "Look, Lindsay, I know this isn't the type of thing you typically talk about with anyone, let alone a guy you just met yesterday, but I need to know what the odds are here. I can't stand waiting for weeks without knowing. I want to be as mentally prepared as possible for whatever the outcome is."

Something flashes in his eyes I can't quite pin down before he schools his expression. Maybe sadness?

"I guess I can understand where you're coming from. So, to answer your earlier question, my period ended about a week ago, so I think we're safe by about a week."

"You don't start counting at the end. It starts on the day you start. You can ovulate as early as day ten. We may not be as safe as you think we are." He stares at me expectantly.

I rub my hand against my face and sigh. This is too fucking weird. I can't believe I've let myself get into this position.

"Well, I don't know exactly where I'm at then. I've never really had to worry about it before, so I don't really pay attention. I wait for the zit that appears without fail, and the cramps. I don't know what to tell you. We'll have to wait and see what happens in a few weeks," I say with a shrug. "How do you know so much about all this female reproductive shit anyway?" It's weird.

It's Rhett's turn to sigh and scrub his hands against his face and into his hair. "I guess it's only fair to tell you something personal about me since I've grilled you about all that. Which, by the way, we're not done. You're going to figure out when you started, but for now, I'll back off." He blows out a deep breath and looks at his hand wrapped around his now-empty beer bottle.

"My ex and I were trying to have a baby. Well, I was anyway. After six months of nothing, I started studying up on the best ways to get pregnant." He finally looks up at me, and I can tell there's a whole hell of a lot more to this story.

As I'm trying to decide if I should ask for more details, he resolves to get it off his chest.

"Lindsay, I've never told anybody about this, but I feel like I can trust you, and for the first time in over a year, I feel like I need to get it out."

"Rhett, you don't have to tell me anything. It's clearly not something easy to talk about, but if you want to, I'm happy to listen, and you can trust me to keep it to myself." I grab his hand from the tabletop and give it a reassuring squeeze.

He gives me a small smile and a nod. "Thanks, sugar. I think I'm going to need another beer."

Before he can move, I jump up and grab him another. Before I sit back down, I place a soft kiss against his lips. When I sit, he takes another deep breath.

"So after the first six months, I tracked everything, desperately trying to get the stars to line up, but still nothing. After another six months, I went to get my shit checked to see if I was the problem. My ex, Amy, was pretty convinced we needed to keep trying and refused to get checked herself, but I couldn't sit back anymore. I wanted a baby so badly. So I went and jacked off in a cup, and let me tell you, it's not like it looks in the movies. No room with porn to get you there, no lube. I had to go to a normal lab where they draw blood and shit and they put me in an exam room with pictures of kids on the wall and hand me a cup and tell me to leave it in this little hole in the wall once I've made my 'deposit.'

"The results came back fine. In fact, they came back better than fine. Apparently, I've got super spooge or something. So the doctor tells me I'm not the problem; I should convince my ex to get tested. When I tried to talk to her about it, she blew me off. Finally, after a couple of weeks, I pinned her down and made her talk to me about it. Then she told me she'd been on birth control the entire time."

"Oh, my God, Rhett. That's awful."

"I was so pissed, I told her to get the fuck out. I grabbed my keys and took off. I came back three days later to my house trashed, but she was gone, and I haven't heard from her since."

"How long were you guys together?"

"Five years."

STEVIE LEE

"Were you married?"

"No, she was very anti-marriage, which was fine by me. I've never been very traditional. I guess she was anti-baby too. She failed to share it with me."

Rhett looks up from his lap, where he's been staring at his hands while he talks. My heart shatters for him. He looks so defeated. His story confuses me a little though. It explains how he knows so much about ovulation and such, but it doesn't entirely explain why he's so adamant about narrowing down the odds of me becoming pregnant from our slipups. I can't decide if he's hoping I will be or not. All I know for sure is I've got to get the look off his face.

I crawl onto Rhett's lap, straddling him. I take his face in my hands and kiss him gently, pouring as much emotion as I can into it. He wraps his arms around my back, holding me tightly against him, and deepens the kiss. It isn't feverish like our others have been. This one is slow and sweet and, dare I say, almost loving.

When we break, I continue to hold his face in my palms so he'll look at me. "I'll do whatever you need of me to set your mind at ease. Do you have a calendar, so I can try to figure out when my last period started?"

Rhett holds me to him and leans forward to retrieve his phone from his back pocket. After a couple of taps to the screen, he hands it to me. Thinking back on the last couple of weeks, I figure out I'm on about day twelve or thirteen. After telling Rhett my conclusion, he nods and sets me on my feet. After a too-brief hug and planting a kiss on top of my head, he walks out of the cabin and into the rain. I watch him through the window as he walks in the direction of the water. I let him go so he can work through whatever's on his mind. What a shitty way to wind up after our mind-blowing sex in the rain.

Rhett doesn't return until after I've finished cooking dinner and sat down to eat alone. I'm halfway through my meal when he steps through the door, his clothing soaked through. He stays put on the rug at the door and pulls off his muddy boots.

Somehow, the way his wet shirt clings to his body is almost sexier than when he's shirtless. Almost. Water drips from his short hair and runs down his face.

There's still a slight trace of sadness in his eyes, but his walk in the rain seems to have cleansed most of it away.

"Go ahead and strip down there. I'll throw your clothes in the wash while you go take a shower to warm up and put some dry clothes on. I'll have a hot plate ready for you when you're done."

He nods before pulling his shirt over his head and handing it to me. "If you wanted to see me naked, sugar, all you had to do was ask," he says with a forced smirk. He's trying to distract me from his sour mood, but I see right through him. That Amy chick really did a number on him, and our reckless behavior made him dredge it to the surface.

"All right, hot shot, get out of those wet clothes. I'm willing to bet you're not nearly as sexy when you're sick."

He scoffs. "Of course I am. Nothing can tone down this level of sexiness."

He hands me his pants as he walks toward the bedroom. I smack his ass as he walks past me. "Joke all you want, Rhett, but I'm not sure even you can pull off a snotty nose!"

His loud laughter echoes through the small cabin.

CHAPTER 8

After changing for bed, I walk up the hallway toward the living room, my bare feet almost silent on the hardwood floors. Rhett is sitting on the couch, hunched over and completely engrossed in his phone. I'm approaching him from behind, thinking it would be funny to startle him, when I notice the pictures he's scrolling through.

Someone poorly photoshopped my face onto erotic images of women in submissive positions. In the next picture, I'm pumping gas while in uniform. Another is of my house with the words "we see you" across it. Me at the grocery store. At the diner with Tenille.

I feel lightheaded, and acid churns in my stomach. I grab onto the back of the couch to steady myself, alerting Rhett to my presence. He quickly blackens his screen but not before I see *#DieLindsayBitch* captioned on one photo.

Rhett stands and turns toward me with a forced smile. "Hey, sugar, ready for bed?"

"What was that on your phone?" The words rasp up my dry throat.

"Ah, nothing. Just a text from my brother." He shrugs and tosses it onto the couch.

"Don't fucking lie to me, Rhett. I saw those pictures and the hashtag. How the fuck did you find that?" My voice is tight, and my hands tremble.

GREENLIGHT

He rubs his hands along his face and into his hair, leaving them on top of his head while he stares at me with apprehension.

"I've had my sister monitor your social media accounts to see if there was any activity on them. Also, you need a stronger password. Kelly hacked your account in like five seconds. Don't you know you're not supposed to use your dog's name?"

I roll my eyes in irritation. "I get it. Who cares? Get to the point."

"You got a new follower on Instagram she thought could be linked to ZMC, so she followed them back out of curiosity. Her request was approved almost immediately, so whoever is behind the account is watching it closely. There are about twenty photos posted much like the screenshots you saw."

I draw my lips between my teeth and nod. "Were you planning to tell me?"

His guilty expression is all the answer I need. He was going to keep it to himself. I don't understand why. Wouldn't he want me to know what I'm up against?

I'm irritated and scared. And now I'm worried I can't trust him, but I don't have a choice. I'm stuck here with no way to leave and nowhere to go if I could. Those images are proof I'm not safe in my own home.

"You know what? I don't want to talk about this. I'm going to bed."

"Lindsay," Rhett calls after me, but I wave my hand in a dismissive gesture and keep moving.

I lie on my side with my back toward the middle of the bed.

Rhett crawls in behind me and lays his hand on my shoulder. "For what it's worth, I'm sorry. I didn't want to tell you because you're safe, and I don't want you stressing over this right now. Keith told me you're a bit of a workaholic and this is a good opportunity for you to disconnect a bit."

I sigh. "It's fine, Rhett. Go to sleep. I'll get over it soon enough. It's just raw right now."

The bed shifts with his movement as he settles in. Thankfully, he listens and leaves me to my thoughts.

I have enjoyed the reprieve from my usual daily grind. I don't think I would have ever done this if it wasn't forced upon me, so I guess there's the silver lining to this situation. But I've allowed the chemistry and attraction with Rhett to cloud my judgement and distract me from the real issue. What happens to my life now?

I've never heard of a gang deciding to renege on a hit. It gets carried out, or they keep searching. In either case, I'm fucked. I could continue to run. Quit my job and reinvent myself... but how long will it last? I'll be looking over my shoulder constantly, and that's no way to live.

Maybe I can come to some sort of truce with Hammond. I give up my K-9 position and stop interrupting their business, and they let me live. I could go back to my old position. Do my eight and hit the gate. Head down, no waves, just survival.

Tears spring in my eyes. I hate that idea. I'd have to give up Kody. He's my partner, but he's owned by the department, and they won't give him up until he's ready to retire. Some other handler will step up in my place.

I'm scared and feeling defeated. I have no answers. I'm forced to sit back and wait until somebody tells me where to go from here. It's an awful feeling for a woman who has prided herself on being strong and independent. Even worse, I feel safest when I'm in Rhett's arms. It's stupid because I don't really know him. The feminist voice in my head screams I don't need a man, but a part of me wants this one.

The uncertainty and complete lack of control sets my nerves on edge, and the tears I'd managed to hold back streak down my cheeks. I cover my mouth with both hands, trying to choke back the sobs caught in my throat. My body vibrates with the effort. I take deep, shuddering breaths to calm my emotions. I don't want Rhett to see my vulnerability.

It's all in vain though. Rhett pulls me against his chest and holds tight as I struggle to push him away. I don't want his comfort; he was going to lie to me.

    He gently squeezes me in his arms and whispers, "Let go, sugar. I've got you. You're safe with me, I promise. Let me hold you."

    The fight drains out of me. I don't have enough energy to fight both his comfort and the demons in my head. If I'm being honest, I need this more than I will ever admit out loud. I'm spiraling, and his quiet embrace is the only thing holding me together.

CHAPTER 9

I'm alone in bed when the sun brightens the room. I let Rhett hold me, my back to his chest, until his breathing slowed and evened out. We didn't talk much, all our words superficial. He kept trying to be funny to lighten the mood, but he gave up when he realized I wasn't buying it.

His absence tells me he's still feeling somber this morning, and he needs a little more time to himself. The note I find next to a freshly brewed pot of coffee confirms my suspicions.

Lindsay, I decided to go fishing this morning to clear my head. I'll be back in a few hours, hopefully with dinner. :) xo, Rhett

I make myself some toast and a cup of coffee before walking to my favorite tree at the edge of the clearing. I'm careful with my steps, making a quiet approach, hoping to see some deer or elk.

I sit there through most of the morning, seeing nothing more than a few squirrels and birds. No matter, it killed time and gave me something to look at other than the blank walls of the cabin. My growling stomach reminds me I haven't had anything more than toast and coffee in hours, and I doubt Rhett has had anything at all. He would've had to walk right by me if he'd returned from fishing, so I know he's not been back for lunch.

With a sandwich, a bag of chips, and a couple of bottles of water, I find Rhett sitting atop the dirt berm of the dam on the far end of the lake.

"Hey, sugar, what brings you out here?" he asks as I sit on the still-damp ground beside him.

"I wanted to bring you some lunch. I won't stay. I wanted to make sure you ate and were still alive."

"Thanks, baby," he says, taking the food from me and pressing a sweet kiss against my lips. "Not just for the food but for giving me my space too. It's nothing personal against you. I need the quiet to clear my head of the shit our conversation stirred up yesterday. And last night."

"I know, I get it. You don't have to explain yourself to me. I think we both needed a little space this morning. Yesterday was heavy. I only showed up out here to bring you food. I'll let you get back to your fishing," I say as I stand and brush off my butt. I wrinkle my nose at the dampness I feel. Rhett chuckles and stands.

"You're too cute. Come here and give me a kiss before you go." Rhett pulls me against himself before joining our mouths. Our kiss doesn't get hot and heavy. It's a show of affection. I've never had this level of attraction before. I'm not usually the touchy-feely type, but with Rhett, I could get used to this.

When Rhett returns a few hours later, he sets to work cleaning the fish he caught and makes me dinner. We share easy conversation about our jobs and our lives like two people getting to know each other on a first date.

Afterward, I do the dishes and clean up the kitchen, while Rhett does push-ups and sit-ups to burn off a little excess energy before jumping in the shower. I'm a little bummed I'm not able to watch his powerful muscles flexing under the strain of his body's own weight. I'll have to settle for my imagination this time.

Shortly after I hear the shower start, I hear the unmistakable reverberation of a gunshot.

I bolt upright in my seat and see the beams of a truck's headlights bouncing through the trees down the two-track road leading to the cabin. The raindrops on the window glisten and blur my view slightly. The ZMC must have found me and shot the lock off the gate.

I swallow down the bile creeping up my throat. Before my panic can fully set in, I jump from the couch and run to the bedroom to grab my pistol.

I ease the slide back enough to ensure there's a round in the chamber. I've only got six rounds, so I've got to make each shot count. I don't know how many men Hammond would send to take me out, but I'm hoping I'll be able to fend them off until Rhett can help.

I duck behind the couch, where I can keep an eye on the truck's progression down the road through the window. It doesn't make the best form of cover, but at least I'm concealed from view.

As the truck gets closer, I realize they're going to get here a lot sooner than I hoped for. They're driving down the rutted road like a bat out of hell, their headlights jumping wildly through the darkness. Whoever is driving is in a hurry to get here, probably hoping to catch me off guard.

I wipe the nervous sweat from my palms onto my pants and readjust my grip on my pistol to stare unblinking out the window at the quickly approaching beams of light.

"What the fuck are you doing?"

I about jump out of my skin. I was so focused on the truck, I didn't hear Rhett walking up the hallway behind me. "Son of a bitch, you scared the shit out of me!" Of course he's standing there in only a towel, and I can't take the time to appreciate his gorgeous body. "Would you go to put some fucking clothes on and grab your gun?"

"Grab my gun? I've got a gun for you right here, baby." He's grabbing himself through the towel. If it were any other time, I might be slightly amused, but right now, I need him to get his damn pistol and help me figure out a way to get out of here without getting shot or kidnapped.

"Somebody shot the lock off the gate." I gesture out the window toward the road.

His smile fades as he realizes the gravity of the situation. Before I can say anything else, he's running back to the bedroom and comes back out seconds later with his jeans on and his Walther 9mm in his hands.

"How many rounds you got in that thing?" he asks, kneeling beside me.

"Six, I've already got one chambered."

His eyebrows raise like he's surprised I know what I'm talking about. It's easy to pass a weapons qualification. It's another thing to be proficient.

"All right, stay down and cover me. Conserve your shots since you don't have very many. Don't just throw some Hail Marys, make them count. I'm going to sneak over by the door and hope to catch them as they come in. Keep watch out the window and try to figure out how many guys we're dealing with." He grabs my chin and forces me to look into his eyes. "We're going to be all right. You trust me?"

I nod once. I do trust him, completely. He presses a kiss to my lips before pulling away and crawling to the door. As he gets into position, the vehicle pulls to a stop and shuts down. What I assumed to be a truck ends up being a lime-green Jeep Wrangler. Seems a little conspicuous to drive when you're going to murder someone.

Rhett's gaze locks onto me, waiting for any information I can give him.

The inside of the Jeep is dark, and I can barely make out a slight bit of movement inside the cab. I'm holding my breath, and my heart is pounding in my chest. I've dealt with stressful situations in the prison often enough over the past several years without any hesitation, but right now, I'm freaking the fuck out. I guess I never felt like my life was in danger before now.

Inside, I've got plenty of backup. The good guys always win. We might get rattled, but we come out on top. Right here, right now, we're evenly matched. Weapons, manpower… We're miles away from any other person.

I suddenly realize how uneventful my life has been. I've done nothing but work for years. Even when I had a boyfriend, I didn't make the most of the relationship. I've always focused on my career instead of anything else, and now the possibility of never being able to do any of the things normal people do in their lifetime is staring me in the face. I want to do them all. I want to fall in love for real and travel and have a family, and I don't know. Just… just live.

Rhett must sense my panic. His voice breaks through the fog of anxiety.

"Breathe, baby. We're going to be fine. Tell me what you see."

I take a deep steadying breath, focus on the Jeep again, and try to pull out as many details as I can.

"I can't make out more than a bit of movement in the front seat. There's at least two people. They opened the doors, hang on."

I'm watching with rapt attention. The man who got out of the driver's side—if I can call him a man, he looks like he's sixteen years old—jogs around to the front of the Jeep where he's met by a girl. He grabs her around the waist and kisses her deeply. My brow furrows in confusion.

"Talk to me, baby. What do you see?"

"Um, it's a kid and his girlfriend, apparently. They're standing there making out in front of the Jeep. Nobody else seems to be getting out."

"Mother fucker, is the Jeep bright green?"

I nod.

"Jesus fuck, I'm going to kill him." He slips his gun into the back waistband of his jeans and jerks the door open.

I'm even more confused now. What in the world is going on?

"Brandon! What the fuck are you doing here?"

Who is Brandon? I guess I should feel relieved Rhett seems to know who this is and he isn't here to kill me. I get the feeling things are about to get awkward.

I drop the magazine from my gun and rack the round out of the chamber. I replace the shell back into the mag and slam it into the grip. Once my weapon is safely reloaded, I take it back to the bedroom. I take the few minutes of privacy to pull myself together. A few deep breaths and my adrenaline starts to ebb, and I feel like I can breathe easy again.

Rhett comes through the bedroom door cursing. He sets his pistol on his bedside table and strips off his jeans, still muttering under his breath something about "that damn kid" and a "love shack."

I sit on the bed with an amused smirk and watch the show. An angry, naked Rhett is something worth slowing down to take in.

He drags on a pair of boxer briefs and puts his jeans and a T-shirt on. I frown; I like the low-slung-jeans-with-no-underwear look. It's hot.

"What's the matter?"

I drag my eyes up from his abs toward his face. "What?"

"What's the matter? You're frowning at me."

"I was thinking I liked the commando look better. So who's Brandon?" I ask, changing the subject quickly.

"Brandon is Keith's nineteen-year-old son. I figured it wasn't appropriate to free-ball around his little girlfriend. He thought it would be a good idea to sneak up here after classes and spend the weekend fucking, since he still lives at home and she lives in the dorms back at school. I guess they were looking forward to a few days without their roommates interrupting."

I burst out laughing. "I guess we ruined their plans."

Rhett laughs too, and I watch the tension melt out of his shoulders.

It was an intense few minutes of not knowing who was coming down the road. He must have been as nervous as I was, waiting for some psycho to come murder me. But as thankful as I am it wasn't the MC, it's still going to be awkward to have Brandon and his girlfriend here on our last night. I'm curious where those two are going to sleep. I ask Rhett about it.

"Fuck if I know, but I'm sure as hell not giving up the bed. They can sleep in the back of his Jeep for all I care. I can't believe he did this. What the hell was he thinking? Keith is going to fucking kill him for shooting the lock off the gate. And then what was his plan to get into the cabin? Break a goddamned window?"

"I'm guessing he thought this through with the wrong head," I say with a smirk, trying to lighten his mood. While the situation isn't ideal, I'm so relieved the MC isn't here to kill me I can't seem to be upset by Brandon and his girlfriend.

Sure, it's going to be awkward as fuck, but at least we're not engaged in a gun battle with some soulless outlaw the MC sent.

I know I'm trained for such situations, but I don't think it's something anyone can truly prepare for. I'd like to think I could shoot somebody in a kill-or-be-killed situation, but if I'm being completely honest, I'd rather not find out.

Before I can think too much more on it, Rhett wraps me up in his arms and presses his lips to my temple. "You okay? That was scary for a few minutes there."

I lean back a little and look up into his face. His genuine concern and affection stare back at me.

"I'm good. I was scared shitless until they started making out. Thank you for keeping me focused. I was losing it, and you pulled me back to reality. I'm so thankful you're here with me. I feel safer knowing if something goes down, you're going to be able to protect me. You really are capable of fending off more than a drunken cowboy trying to grab Taylor Swift's ass."

He laughs, a hearty deep laugh I can feel vibrate through his chest. "It's nice to know you've had such faith in me this whole time. Let's be honest here though, there aren't any cowboys at a Taylor Swift concert."

It's my turn to laugh. "You're probably right."

Rhett releases me from his embrace, takes me by the hand, and leads me out to the living room. I guess it's time to sort out what to do about our intruders.

We find them huddled together on the couch, whispering to each other heatedly. The girl seems nervous. Brandon appears to be trying to calm her down.

"Uncle Rhett, I'm sorry to show up like this. I didn't know you were up here with someone. We'll pull the air mattress out of the closet and set it up out here for the night. We'll leave in the morning. Can we not tell my dad about this? He's going to fucking kill me if he finds out."

"I'm not going to tell your dad shit, but you are. You shot the lock off the gate. How am I supposed to explain that to your dad?"

"We'll put a different lock on it. I'll go into town in the morning and buy one. He'll never have to know. Please, Uncle Rhett. You were my age once. We wanted a little privacy."

I almost feel sorry for the kid. I can understand wanting some alone time when you're constantly surrounded by your classmates. However, he should've thought this through better.

Rhett seems exasperated with Brandon and scrubs his hand against the scruff on his jaw.

"That's all well and good, kid, but how am I supposed to explain why his key won't open the lock when he comes up here next weekend?"

Brandon looks defeated. It's obvious he hadn't considered the consequences. His focus was aimed for a weekend of fucking without regard for anything else.

I can't stand to listen to them argue about this anymore. Rhett is coming off like an overbearing father, and Brandon is acting like a stupid kid. This is not something I'm up to dealing with. I'm sure all of this will look different in the morning once Rhett and I have completely come down from our adrenaline high and we can all be more reasonable.

"All right, guys. Enough about this tonight. Let's get something to eat, and we'll deal with this in the morning. Rhett, help me cook some dinner, and you two get the air mattress blown up."

"Yes, ma'am," they both mumble. Jesus Christ! Ma'am? I'm not even ten years older than them. Now I feel like I'm the overbearing parent.

We make it through dinner without Rhett killing Brandon, which is a small miracle, considering how angry he'd been.

I'm lying next to Rhett with my head on his chest and my leg thrown over his thighs. The steady beat of his heart lulls me into blissful unconsciousness, but I'm interrupted by the occasional giggle coming from the living room.

"I'm glad we're leaving tomorrow. Brandon can stay up here and answer to Keith whenever." Rhett's irritation is still palpable, so I decide a change of subject is in order.

"What happens tomorrow?" I ask.

"What do you mean? We're going to pick up Shawn from the airport and spend the day either at his hotel or we may go to my house and then we'll be at the concert venue for a good portion of Friday."

"I know all of that. I mean with us. Up here, we've been in our own little world. Has this just been a fling and we pretend it never happened? Are we going to try a relationship? I'm curious where your head's at."

Rhett takes a deep breath. I know he had to have thought about this while he was away all afternoon. I refuse to look at his face, afraid of what I might see. I watch my fingers twirl the hair trailing down from his belly button. Maybe he doesn't want anything to do with me after it's safe for me to go home.

If I think about it, maybe I won't want anything to do with him either. Maybe I should have my fun now and then get back to the way things were.

Who am I kidding? I want everything with him.

"Look, Lindsay. These past few days with you have been amazing. I didn't think I could connect with anybody the way I've connected with you. I thought my chance at happiness walked out the door with Amy, but you've got me all fucked up in the head, and I can't decide what I want to do. I'm afraid to put myself in a position to get hurt like I did before, yet I feel like I've already done that by opening up to you about Amy. And fucking you bareback, I should've known better. I should've kept this strictly professional, but I couldn't. The chemistry I felt between us within the first hour of meeting you was more than I've felt with anybody, ever.

"So to answer your question, I don't know what happens tomorrow or the next day. I do know I'm going to protect you and keep you safe until you can go home and get back to your life. I guess at that point, we can decide where to go from there. And until then, I think we should do whatever comes naturally, with protection."

Wow, that was some statement. It wasn't necessarily the declaration of love or the smack in the face I was expecting, but he was honest, which is all I can ask for.

I don't know what to say. I think I'll go with it and hope we both feel the same way at the end of it all, no matter which way things go. I can't fall in love with him and him kick me to the curb when my situation is said and done. That's the most probable outcome though, I'm sure.

CHAPTER 10

I rise with the sun Thursday morning. Rhett is still peacefully sleeping next to me. I slip out of bed to use the restroom and brush my teeth before he wakes.

I slide back between the sheets and curl up next to his warm body. He wraps his arms around me and pulls me on top of him. His large hands grip my ass and hold my core right over his erection.

With my hands on his chest, I sit astride him and take in the smug smile on his handsome face. I trace my fingertips down his rough jaw and across his full lips. He kisses the pads of my fingers before smacking my ass and lifting me off him to take his turn in the bathroom.

He comes back toward me, stripping his boxers off. I follow suit until I'm naked. He grabs my hips and pulls me on top of him as he falls onto his back. His kisses are rough and passionate. I love the way his beard causes my lips to sting and swell.

He dips a finger into me, testing my wetness before grabbing a condom out of the nightstand and rolling it onto his hard cock. I rise onto my knees so he can position himself beneath me. There is no better feeling than being filled so perfectly. Nothing feels as good as that first slide home.

Once he's fully inside, I sit for a moment to adjust to his size, and a shudder runs through me.

"Good morning, baby." His grin is contagious. I can't help but smile back as I lean forward and kiss him.

He runs his hands down my back and grips my ass, encouraging me to move. I sit back up and rest my hands on his stomach, and I slide up and down his impressive length.

He cups my breasts and pinches my nipples. I arch my back, bringing my hips forward enough to bring contact with my clit against his pubic bone. I feel my orgasm building and know it won't be long before I come crashing down.

I'm seconds away from my orgasm when the bedroom door opens and Brandon and Amber stand frozen, staring at my naked back.

Rhett quickly pulls the sheet over us and pulls me down to his chest to hide my breasts and bare ass from view.

"Get the fuck out!" Rhett bellows at them.

I bury my face in his neck, totally mortified. I had forgotten they were even here.

"We needed to use the bathroom. I didn't think you were awake yet, so we thought we'd sneak in really quick without waking you."

"You can piss outside. There's a whole fucking forest out there, take your pick of tree."

"Fine, I'll go outside, but at least let Amber use the bathroom, so she doesn't have to squat in the bushes."

Brandon's right. It's messed up to make Amber drop trou in the cool morning air when there's a perfectly good toilet nearby. I lift my head enough to look at them and tell her to hurry.

With Amber secured behind the bathroom door and Brandon presumably outside, Rhett kisses my neck and nibbles on my earlobe.

He whispers in my ear, "I know you were about to come when they walked in. Think I can get you off before she walks out?" He continues kissing my neck and thrusts his hips. I have no idea how he maintained his erection through all of that, but he did. I feel like somebody dumped a bucket of ice water on my libido. There is no way I can come back from that before she comes out, and I'd rather not get caught in the act again.

"Sorry, baby, I think the mood's shot." I climb off him, trying my best to keep the sheet over us, but I fail miserably. As my back hits the mattress, the sheet comes with me, completely exposing Rhett in all his latex-glad glory. Amber chooses that exact moment to walk into the room.

She screams an "omigod" and slaps her hands over her eyes and spins around. I can't help it; I burst out laughing. Our luck has been shit this morning. Rhett isn't nearly as amused as I am. He glares at me as he pulls the sheet from me and rearranges it, ensuring we are both covered completely.

"All right, Amber, we're decent. You can turn around now," I say through my laughter so she can cross the room to get to the door.

She turns around and uncovers her eyes but seems to be rooted in place, staring at us. Her face is flush with embarrassment. "I'm really sorry. I didn't see much, I swear." She's found her ability to speak but not her ability to walk, apparently.

"It's fine, just go so we can get up and get dressed, please." I've stopped laughing now and am ready for this to be over.

For some odd reason, she still won't fucking leave. If I were her, I'd have run from the room the second his dick sprang free, but she can't seem to get a hold of herself. Rhett is pissed beside me.

"Fuck it. If she won't leave the room, I will. I'm not going to lie here all fucking day."

Before I can register what he said, Rhett is out of bed and walking across the room toward the bathroom and Amber.

Her eyes stay glued to his dick the entire time. As he walks past her, I hear him mumble, "Get a good look at it, honey," before he disappears into the bathroom and slams the door. I giggle a little.

Amber buries her face in her hands again. "Oh, my god. What the fuck is wrong with me?"

"It's hard not to stare at something so impressive."

She looks at me wide-eyed, clearly shocked I would call her out like that. I wink and nod my head toward the door. She finally takes the hint and leaves the room, then closes the door quietly behind her.

Once Rhett and I are cleaned up and dressed, we head into the kitchen to make coffee. The kids are once again on the couch, whispering. I can only imagine how their conversation is going, and I am damn thankful to not be a part of it.

While the coffee perks, Rhett pushes my back against the counter, holding my hips in his strong hands, and kisses the life out of me.

We're interrupted by Brandon clearing his throat. We both groan as we separate and look at him.

"Uncle Rhett, can I talk to you outside?"

"No, but you can talk to me right here."

Brandon glances from Rhett to me and then back to Rhett. He's clearly irritated he's not getting his way, but Rhett doesn't give him an inch.

"What did you guys say to Amber? She's demanding we leave right now and won't tell me what happened."

Rhett huffs out a laugh. "We didn't say anything to her. She might have seen my dick when she came out of the bathroom and then wouldn't leave the fucking room. She stood there staring at us, so I got up, and I'm certain she saw it that time. I'm guessing she's a little embarrassed to be so entranced by this old guy's dick when she's got a young stud like you in her bed."

Without waiting for a response from Brandon, Rhett turns to the coffee pot and pours us both a cup. He presses another kiss to my mouth before putting the cup in my hands and winks at me.

I can tell he said all that to piss Brandon off. After all, the kid crashed our party this morning. He deserves a little ribbing. Rhett might have been a little harsh, but I can't blame him. That was some spectacular sex we had to walk away from.

Brandon doesn't seem to want to let the conversation end there. "Why would you get out of bed in front of her?"

"She wouldn't leave. I wasn't going to lie in bed all day with a condom on, waiting for her to come to her senses. I needed to get up and take care of shit. I'm sure she'd seen everything by then, so I figured it didn't matter if she saw it again. I'd lost my hard-on, anyway."

Before this can get further out of hand, I decide I'd better intervene. I can't see things getting better. "Rhett and I are going to pack up and head out in about an hour. Why don't you take Amber into town to buy the replacement lock while we get the truck loaded? By the time you get back, we'll be ready to leave, if not gone. Save her a little embarrassment from having to look your uncle in the eye." I can't help the little laugh that slips out.

Brandon nods, and we hear him lead Amber out to the Jeep and drive away.

Rhett wastes no time. He picks me up, sets me on the counter, and spreads my legs wide as he steps between them. He kisses along the column of my neck and up to my mouth. Our tongues tangle together in a passionate, coffee-flavored kiss.

"Should we pick up where we left off? I believe I owe you an orgasm."

He doesn't give me a chance to answer before he scoops me up and carries me back to the bedroom. Once inside, he kicks the door closed and locks it.

"I'll be damned if we get interrupted again. I've got a serious case of blue balls. I'm going to fuck you so hard, you're going to walk funny for the rest of the day."

He doesn't disappoint. I'm deliciously sore as I climb into the passenger seat of his truck an hour later.

On the way out, we catch up to Brandon and Amber pulled over on the side of the road, within view of the cabin. It appears they were waiting for us to leave before returning. Can't say I blame them.

Rhett rolls down his window, and Brandon does the same as we pull up alongside them. Amber stares out her window, never glancing our way. Poor girl must want to crawl in a hole and die after the way she acted this morning.

"You can explain yourself to your dad when we give him the keys to the new lock, and don't think you can get away with not telling him. I'm going to let him know you need to talk to him. I don't want your dad to think he can't trust me with the use of his cabin, but I won't completely throw you under the bus either. Just man-up and tell him the truth. He'll be pissed, but he was also your age once and will understand. Just try to think with your head a little more, and not so much with your dick."

"Uncle Rhett, if I never hear you say 'dick' again, it will be too soon." He reaches his arm out the window toward Rhett to bump fists. "And maybe you should take your own advice there. You're the one who couldn't keep it in your pants this morning," he says with a laugh. It's good to see his sense of humor has returned.

"Touché. I can't help it with this beautiful woman sitting next to me. Don't get in any more trouble this week, and be safe."

Four and a half hours later, we're pulling into the airport to pick up Rhett's cousin, the one and only country superstar Shawn Cross. Nervous excitement churns around in my stomach. I'm silently praying I can keep my dignity and not go complete fangirl on him.

We park in a short-term parking garage, since Shawn's flight won't land for another twenty minutes. I jump from the truck and stretch my cramped, tired limbs. Rhett meets me at the tailgate, wrapping me in a hug for a quick kiss. He holds my hand as we walk toward the terminal.

"When Shawn gets here, we're going to have to hustle out to the truck and hope we don't get mobbed. Hopefully nobody recognizes him, and we can get out of here in one piece. Either way, stay close so I can keep you from getting trampled." Rhett wraps his arm around my shoulder and pulls me close, pressing another kiss to the top of my head. I revel in the way it feels to be against him. A girl could get used to this.

As I stand next to Rhett, daydreaming about all we could be, I notice a tall man wearing a black ball cap pulled down over his eyes. Now when I say tall, I mean really tall. I'd say Rhett is probably six foot, maybe six one. This guy is more like six four and broad shoulders.

The man walks right up to me, grabs my face in his enormous hands, and plants a sloppy kiss to my lips.

I freeze. I don't know what to make of this. Realization slowly dawns on me. This must be Rhett's cousin, Shawn, but it doesn't explain why he's kissing me.

Rhett growls beside me. "Fucking Shawn. Come on, back off, asshole."

Shawn breaks away from me, laughing. He pulls Rhett into a bro hug and slaps him heartily on the back. "I didn't know you were bringing a girl for me. You did good, brother. She's gorgeous!"

I turn my face away to conceal the shit-eating grin I can't keep from spreading across my face. I get the feeling the kiss was more of Shawn trying to get a rise out of Rhett and less to do with an attraction toward me, but I still can't help but be a little affected by it. I mean, he's fucking Shawn Cross. Tenille is going to kill me when she hears about this.

"All right, motherfucker, that's enough. Let's get the fuck out of here before you get recognized and then I'll properly introduce you to Lindsay from the safety of my truck." Rhett grabs my hand and drags me through the airport and out to the truck. He pulls me around to the driver's side of the truck, so I'm thinking I'm going to sit in the back seat and Shawn will ride shotgun. No big deal. I'm the shortest, so it makes sense I'd be the one to ride in the back, but Rhett seems to have other plans.

I pull open the back door and make to climb up inside when I feel Rhett's hands on my hips, pulling me back toward him.

"What do you think you're doing?" he whispers into my ear.

I turn to look at his face. I want to get a read on his expression. I know he's a little fired up about Shawn kissing me, but I'm hoping his anger isn't directed at me.

I'm relieved to see he's not angry at all, more like mischievous. Maybe even a little predatory. Looks like Shawn's little stunt brought out the caveman in Rhett. I like it… a lot. His hands are still gripping my hips, and he's pulling them in toward his. I feel a slight stirring beneath the zipper of his jeans. I'm melting into him in the parking garage of the airport with my mind void of anything but the feelings he's stirring within me.

"What do you mean? I'm getting in the truck so we can get out of here."

He pulls me out of the way, slams the back door, and pulls the front door open. Shawn grins at me as he lifts the center console to create a bench seat. He settles his arm across the back of the middle seat and winks at me suggestively.

"I can't sit there. My legs are too long. You won't be able to shift."

Rhett and Shawn laugh. "I can shift fine with you sitting there. I want you next to me. Now climb up there."

I do as he asks, and he smacks my ass as I crawl into the cab of the truck. While I'm squished up next to Shawn, he wraps his long fingers around my knee and squeezes, making me jump a little.

"See, you fit fine. We just have to get a little friendly is all. I certainly don't mind pressing up against you like this. If you need more room while he's shifting, just take it. I don't want him to bruise your knees; I'm sure it would put a damper on things later tonight," Shawn says with a salacious grin.

"Jesus Christ, Shawn. Shut the fuck up and get your damn hand off her knee. I didn't bring her along for you to be pawing all over." As if Rhett remembers his manners, he sighs and makes introductions. "Lindsay, meet my cousin, country superstar and man-whore, Shawn Cross. Shawn this is Lindsay Lanier."

"It's very nice to meet you, lovely Lindsay," Shawn says, shaking my hand. "Now tell me, what are you to Rhett? He made sure to add several adjectives to my introduction, but he was exceedingly vague with yours."

Oh, shit. What the hell am I supposed to say? We haven't given ourselves a label. I wouldn't say we are in a relationship, since our time together has a quickly approaching expiration date. I don't really want to say I am the girl Rhett is fucking either. For one, it doesn't paint me in a particularly good light, and two, I would like to think what we had going was more than just fucking. At least, it feels that way to me.

The silence in the truck stretches and becomes uncomfortable. I can't help but notice Rhett isn't saying anything either. It's the moment when neither of us wants to say the wrong thing and complicate our already-strange situation. I decide I should leave the physical portion of our relationship out of the conversation. It isn't any of Shawn's business, and I don't feel like it's relevant.

"We met through a mutual friend. He's my knight in shining armor, I guess you could say. I've gotten myself into a little bit of a dangerous situation at work, and Rhett has stepped in to make sure I'm safe until it's all handled and I'm good to return to my duties."

There, that seems innocent enough. I chance a glance at Rhett, and he gives me a grateful smile. I guess he didn't want his cousin to know about us fucking either. I can't help my slight tinge of disappointment. A part of me wanted him to correct me and say we are together or something, but he didn't. I know better than to think that, but a girl can want.

"Where are we headed, Shawn? You got a room booked somewhere, or are we going to the house?"

The tone of Rhett's voice was a little tight. I doubt Shawn noticed, but after spending the last few days getting to know Rhett, I can't help but read the emotion on his face and in his voice like a book. I think the slight discussion of our status upset him. More disappointment surges through me.

My return to reality is going to hurt. I am falling for him, and it is beginning to feel like he doesn't feel the same about me.

When we were alone, he was easygoing and sweet, and I could almost see us moving toward relationship territory when everything blows over. But now that we are with his cousin, it feels like his entire attitude shifted. I wish I knew what it was about. I don't think I am going to get a chance to ask him though. Turns out Shawn doesn't want to stay in a hotel. He wanted to stay at Rhett's until he had to be at the concert venue.

After a quick stop at the grocery store and a *carniceria* to pick up the fixings for tacos, at Shawn's request, we pulled up to Rhett's.

Rhett's house is a large, two-story farmhouse with a wrap-around porch, gray with white trim. There is a detached three-car garage that looks like it has an apartment or something above it. It all sits on what I guess is about two-and-a-half acres of well-maintained land. I'm impressed. It isn't exactly what I'd consider a bachelor pad.

"Shawn, why don't you take the room downstairs? I'll take Lindsay upstairs to her room so she can settle in. I'll be back in a few minutes to fire up the grill. There should be beer in the fridge."

Shawn nods and disappears down a hallway toward the back of the house, while Rhett takes to the stairs and I follow closely. At the top, he grabs my hand and leads me into the master bedroom. He sets our bags on top of his dresser, pulls me into his arms, and kisses me sweetly.

"You okay?" I ask him. "You've seemed a little off since we picked up Shawn. Aren't you happy to see him?"

"I'm fine. I just let him get to me a little; that's all. Come on, let's go cook dinner." Rhett tries to pull me from the room, but I stand firm. He turns toward me and raises his eyebrows.

"What do you mean you let him get to you?"

"Shawn is always a flirt, but he's never flirted with a girl I was with, and I guess I got a little jealous when he set his sights on you."

I laugh. He can't possibly think Shawn was genuinely flirting with me. It was solely to get a rise out of Rhett. Even I figured that out right away. Apparently, it worked.

This time, I grab his hand and lead him from the room. When we reach the stairs, I plant a kiss against his cheek and look him straight in the eyes. "You have nothing to be jealous about. I don't want Shawn."

We find Shawn in the kitchen setting groceries on the counter and prepping for our taco night. Rhett goes out a set of french doors off the kitchen to light the grill, and I sidle up to Shawn to help with everything else.

"He all right?" Shawn asks with a nod of his head toward the back deck. "I heard you talking right now."

"Yeah, he's fine. Maybe feeling a little insecure but he has nothing to worry about."

"Aw, come on now! You don't want to have a wild night with a famous country music singer?"

At that exact moment, Rhett walks back inside. He stops dead in his tracks and looks between Shawn and me.

I shake my head and laugh. "Not a chance, hot shot." I wrap my arms around Rhett's neck and plant a smacking kiss to his cheek.

He grabs the backs of my thighs, right beneath my ass, and lifts me so I can wrap my legs around his waist. Setting me on the edge of the counter, he kisses me deeply. He has one hand buried in my hair and the other braced against my lower back, pressing my heat against the bulge growing behind his zipper. My breasts rub deliciously against his chest, causing my nipples to pebble.

All presence of mind leaves me as I lose myself in Rhett—until Shawn opens his damn mouth.

"Goddamn, that is so fucking hot! Although, I wish I wasn't watching my cousin. You know what, fuck it, keep going."

"Jesus Christ, Shawn. Can't you keep your fucking mouth shut?" Rhett shoots a glare at Shawn, but we're both laughing.

"I could, but it's more fun watching you go all alpha on the poor girl. I got it, you've staked your claim, marked your territory. Just do us all a favor and don't piss on her."

"Maybe she's into that sort of thing. Ever think of that?"

"Okay, okay! That's enough of that! Nobody is peeing on me! The whole alpha-male thing is superhot, but if anybody tries to pee on me, I'll break your dick in half."

Both men groan and grab themselves. I can't help but giggle.

While Rhett grills the marinated meat outside, Shawn and I work together to make taco fixings. I shred cabbage, and Shawn chops onion, tomato, and cilantro to make pico de gallo.

"So, this thing with you and Rhett. It's serious?" Shawn asks me.

I don't know how to answer him. I'm sure things look serious when we're all over each other and Rhett is acting all territorial, but I get the feeling his behavior has more to do with competing with his cousin than his actual feelings for me. It's not my place to say that to Shawn though.

"I wouldn't say it's serious yet. We just met a few days ago."

"Then what would you say? Because I know my cousin, and I've never seen him act this way with a woman."

"Not even Amy?" I can't help but ask. I'm curious about the woman who broke Rhett so completely. He told me a lot about the end of their relationship but not much else. I guess it's not really something you talk about with the woman you've just met and started fucking.

Shawn looks shocked. "He told you about Amy?"

"He told me a little about her. More like mentioned he hadn't been in a relationship since her."

Shawn stares at me with a contemplative look. I can tell he's trying to decide how much to tell me, if anything at all, without betraying his cousin.

"He loved Amy, but he wasn't smitten with her like he is with you.

STEVIE LEE

I think it was easier staying with her than breaking up and dealing with the fallout, so they just comfortably existed together for most of their relationship. I still don't know the entire story of why they broke up. I think she cheated on him or something."

I work hard to keep my face neutral since I know infidelity wasn't why they ended—but something much worse. Rhett must not want anybody to know. I feel privileged he trusted me with something so personal. He didn't even tell Shawn, who is not only his cousin but his best friend. Looks like the perfect time for a subject change.

"What about you, Mr. Country Music Superstar? Are you seeing anybody?" I bump his shoulder with mine. Well, more like his bicep. The dude is fucking tall.

"Nah, there's no way I could maintain a relationship at this point in my career. I'm on the road ten months out of the year, and the other two I spend in the studio recording. Not to mention the fact there is easy pussy everywhere I look. I think I'll keep taking advantage for a while longer," Shawn says with a wink.

I wrinkle my nose in disgust. "You're going to end up a diseased superstar."

"Fuck no! I always wrap my shit. Always! I won't even let a girl give me head without a rubber. I don't take any chances. And I make sure I deal with the condom when we're done. I don't need some bitch trying to scoop my spooge out, thinking she can get herself a little Shawn in the baby oven. I run across some crazy-ass women out on the road."

"Wow. I don't know what to say. Do you think you'll ever turn loose of the playboy lifestyle?"

Shawn laughs, but it's obvious his lifestyle wears him down a little. He shrugs. "Yeah, in a couple of years maybe. I'm not really a superstar yet. Rhett just likes to bust my balls about it. I'm gaining popularity, but I'm still not making a lot of money yet. My band and I rent a house together in Nashville. My truck was given to me as a promotion for a dealership; otherwise, I'd barely be able to make a payment for a truck like that. The first two songs I've released as singles have done well on the charts, but I'm still waiting for my first number one. My album releases in a few weeks, and I'm just praying it's well received. If I can get my career solid, then I'd like to find a beautiful woman to share this life with."

"I don't follow bands closely or anything, but I know your music. Of course, my best friend is obsessed with you, so she's forced me to listen to every little stitch of music she can find of yours."

"Obsessed, huh? Is she pretty? Do I get to meet this best friend of yours? I could use some ego stroking this stop. Maybe another kind of stroking too."

I laugh. "Of course she's pretty, but she'd probably fall into the crazy category if she ever saw you in person. In fact, she's probably going to kill me when she finds out I met you."

The thought depresses me a bit. Because of this crazy situation I'm in, I've met one man I really like and another my best friend would kill to meet, and I can't share this with her at all. I'm completely cut off from the one person who sees me through everything. I have to admit I'm a little homesick for my best friend.

Normally, I work so much I don't see her often, but I know when I make the time, she'll be around. I don't make the time as often as I should, and I'm seeing it plain as day now. When I get back home, that changes. I'm not taking Tenille for granted anymore. I'm going to be a better friend and make her a greater priority in my life.

Shawn's voice cuts through the fog. "Hey, where'd you go?"

"Um, what?"

"You were talking about your crazy, pretty friend, and you zoned out."

"Oh, sorry. I was just thinking about how my job has stepped on my friendship with Tenille yet again."

"Do you want her to come to the concert? I can get her tickets and backstage passes."

I feel my face light up. It would be so amazing to have Tenille there with me. I know she has tickets, but she'd be thrilled with backstage passes. Before I can reply, Rhett steps into the kitchen with a tray of steaming-hot steak and tortillas.

"She can't have any contact with anybody from home until the threat against her gets resolved. So you won't be able to charm your way into Lindsay's best friend's pants this time."

Way to burst both of our bubbles. Neither Shawn nor I respond. We just quietly set everything out to assemble our tacos.

CHAPTER 11

After we finish dinner and clean up the kitchen, the boys head outside. Apparently, it's a tradition whenever they get together to build a fire, break out guitars, and drink plenty of beer. It surprised me to learn Rhett knows how to play, and quite well from what Shawn had to say. He'd even tried to talk Rhett into playing in his band but hadn't been able to tempt him.

The boys settle in with their beer, and I sip on a bottle of water. I want a beer, but it isn't worth the risk if I really am pregnant. I'd never forgive myself if I indulged and something happened to the baby. After everything Rhett went through with Amy, I don't want to add to his heartache. I know I'm being ridiculously over-cautious, but whatever.

I lean back in my chair and stretch my legs toward the fire, crossing my ankles. I watch the flames as they lick around the mesquite logs within the fire pit, and I listen to its cracks and pops while Rhett and Shawn tune their guitars.

The night is warm, so we're sitting a comfortable distance from the fire but close enough I can still see them both clearly in its glow.

"What should we sing first? Got any requests, Lindsay?" Rhett asks as he strums a few random chords.

"Hmmm, I don't know. What can you play?" I ask.

They both bark out a laugh, like I missed some joke.

"Sweetheart, we can pick our way through just about anything if we try hard enough." Shawn stares me down with a smug smile.

"All right, how about 'Strawberry Wine'?"

"Are you singing? I'm not sure we can do Deanna justice," Shawn says.

"Hell no! I'm not singing in front of you!"

They chuckle but strum and sing the opening line anyway. Three bars in, I quietly sing along with them. I grew up listening to this song. It came out before I could understand what it meant, but I loved it anyway. I remember thinking thirty did seem old, but looking at Rhett, there isn't anything about him that's old.

He's young and carefree, strumming his guitar and singing the song I chose. They switch up the lyrics slightly, to sing from a male perspective, but it is perfect—just like the man I've been sharing a bed with the past few nights. I think I'm falling a little harder tonight.

As the final chord echoes through the night, I reach out and squeeze Rhett's hand resting on the body of the guitar. "Thank you," I whisper to him. He squeezes back and shoots me a wink.

Shawn picks through the intro to a song I recognize.

"Since Lindsay started our night off old-school, I think I'll slow it down and take it back a little further with this one."

Shawn starts singing Keith Whitley's version of "When You Say Nothing at All," and Rhett quickly takes his lead and joins in. I love this song. I slouch in my chair, rest my head back, and bask in the harmony created by two of the sexiest men I have ever laid eyes on.

Tingles shiver down my spine, and goose bumps break out across my arms as they drag out the last note.

"Y'all are going to have to excuse me. I need to go inside and change my panties after that performance."

The boys break out into raucous laughter, but to be honest, I'm only half joking. There is nothing like sitting between two gorgeous, talented men while they serenade you in front of a bonfire on a quiet desert night.

I feel like I should pinch myself to ensure I'm not dreaming. If someone had told me a week ago I'd be sitting here with a man who seems to be smitten with me and his country-music-star cousin while they sang for just me, I'd never believe it. Stuff like this doesn't happen to me. After Ryan and I broke up, men didn't even bat an eye my way. It was like having a failed relationship with a coworker made me a leper or something.

I've spent the last few years existing but not really living. I haven't connected with anyone in so long, I've forgotten what it feels like to enjoy the company of another person. A man.

Any time I've spent with Tenille has always felt forced and uncomfortable, even though she's the best friend I've got. The only friend I've got, really. The pressure she always puts on me to be more social and to jump back into the world of dating has put a strain on our friendship. I love her to death, but I don't need her to be hard on me. I'm hard enough on myself.

I'm broken from my thoughts when Rhett picks through the opening notes of my favorite Garth Brooks song. A huge smile breaks out across my face, and I sit up to pay full attention to his performance. This is going to be a night I'll never forget.

Shawn sang the first verse of "Friends in Low Places," but when Rhett joined in on the chorus, he really did destroy my panties when his voice dropped for the "low" note. My mind frantically searches for a song I can request that would force him to sing with that sexy bass, but I find myself dumbstruck. I can't form a complete thought at all.

I come out of my stupor and realize Rhett is walking away, back toward the house. Before I know what I'm doing, I shout, "Josh Turner!"

Rhett stops in his tracks and turns around to face me. "What?"

I slap my hand over my mouth, mortified. "Never mind! Carry on with whatever it is you're doing."

His eyebrows raise, and he laughs a little as he continues walking away.

"So, the baritone turns you on, huh?" Shawn stares at me with mirth written on his face.

I say nothing, deciding the safest place to look right now is into the fire and to pretend I hadn't given myself away.

"You either want him to sing a Josh Turner song so you can hear that seductive baritone of his, or you want him to sing about being your man, or both. So which is it?" Shawn isn't going to let me pretend I didn't just make a fool of myself.

"The former. I hadn't even considered the song choice when I blurted that out. I'd be foolish to think of him being 'my man' at this point. We're just having a good time while it lasts. But to answer your question, yes, his deep voice is a definite turn-on. Does that make you jealous?"

Shawn's voice is sexy, but it's not as deep as Rhett's. He really doesn't have a reason to be jealous, but it's fun to poke at him a little.

"Jealous of his voice? No. Jealous he's the one who turns you on? Yeah, maybe a little." There's not an ounce of jest to his voice. He's serious. I'm shocked. And this got awkward.

"I'm not sure what I'm supposed to say to that," I say, looking away from him.

"I'm sorry if I made you uncomfortable. I didn't quite mean it the way it came out. I don't necessarily mean you specifically. More like a woman like you. I know you think this thing you and Rhett have is short term and casual, but you're wrong. Rhett doesn't do that kind of relationship. He doesn't sleep around; he's not out looking for the flavor of the week. When he's with a woman, he's looking at a future with her, even in the beginning. He wouldn't waste his time if he didn't think it was going to go somewhere.

"I know I just met you a couple of hours ago, but I can already see what Rhett sees in you. You're the kind of woman a man wants to marry, not the kind he's looking to screw around with and discard. So you can tell yourself this is casual and not going anywhere all you want, but I can guarantee Rhett won't let you go so easily." He finishes the last couple swallows of what I guess is warm beer and stands. "I'm going to head in and get some sleep. It's been a long day." He points at where Rhett is walking back toward us with a glass in his hand. "Make him sing you that song and then make sure he takes care of you. If he doesn't satisfy you, you know where to find me. I won't leave you disappointed," he says with a wink.

"Fuck off, Shawn. I'll make sure she's plenty satisfied. She won't be needing anything from you." Rhett playfully smacks Shawn on the arm.

"I'll back off for now. Sing her that song, bro. I'll see you in the morning." Shawn lumbers off into the darkness, leaving Rhett and me alone with the dying embers of the fire.

Rhett hands me a glass of sweet tea and settles back into his chair with his guitar in his lap. "Josh Turner, huh? All right, I can do that for you."

I hide my shy smile behind my glass of tea and watch him with half-lidded eyes. I told myself I was falling a little harder tonight, but after this, I'll be fucking done for.

Rhett and I drag ourselves into the kitchen in search of coffee. Our late night of love-making left us exhausted.

We're greeted with a chipper and not-the-least-bit-hungover Shawn standing at the stove cooking breakfast.

"Good morning, love birds! I figured you guys probably worked up an appetite last night and could use a solid breakfast to get you through the day. I know I could use an extra energy boost. I didn't get shit for sleep, thanks to you two. You were so fucking loud; I was tempted to come join you. Maybe next time I will." Shawn laughs mischievously while he turns a few pieces of bacon in a frying pan.

My jaw drops a little. Join us? He doesn't look like he's joking, but he has to be... I glance at Rhett to check his reaction. His jaw is a little tense, and he shoots an amused glare at Shawn.

"Don't look at me like that, Rhett. It wouldn't be the first time we've shared a girl," Shawn says, pointing the tongs at Rhett.

My eyes grow wide.

"Jesus fuck, Shawn!" Rhett growls.

"You guys have been in a threesome together?" My curiosity has gotten the better of me. I need to hear this story.

Shawn's eyes sparkle in amusement while Rhett's look a little stormier.

"You want to tell her, or should I?" Rhett glares harder at Shawn. "We fucked the same girl at a party one night when we were in high school. Not at the same time," Rhett tells me, although he won't look at me while he speaks.

He's uncomfortable talking about this. Maybe he's afraid of how I'll react. Honestly, I don't care about his past. I decide to lighten the mood.

"I see. So who got the sloppy seconds then?"

Shawn's laughter fills the kitchen. Rhett's face breaks into a smile. Mission accomplished! The tension evaporates.

Shawn points to his own chest. "That would be me. Rhett walked out with this dazed look on his face and pointed back into the room and said, 'She's willing if you want a turn.' I was like sixteen, so I wasn't turning down willing pussy."

"You act like you've changed. You'd do the same thing today if the opportunity presented itself. Don't try to convince Lindsay you've got morals now. I'm sure she can see right through you."

I don't follow celebrity gossip, but Tenille seriously loves Shawn and analyzes every stitch she can get her hands on, trying to figure out what is truth. Of course, she bounces all her theories off of me, so I've heard a thing or two about Shawn's playboy reputation.

"No judgement from me. You're a country music superstar. Being a slut is part of your job description, right?" I ask with a laugh.

CHAPTER 12

The atmosphere here is amazing. The energy is contagious. I can't help but relax and have a good time. I highly recommend seeing a concert from stageside. The only black spot on my day has been the absence of Tenille. This is something I should be experiencing with her. I'm sure she's out there somewhere in the crowd, having a good time, even though I've unintentionally ditched her again.

I know I'm not supposed to have any contact with her, but after everything I've been through, I need my best friend. I need her to experience this with me, even if I can only sneak her into the after party. She should be able to blend in. I overheard Shawn giving instructions to one of Rhett's men on what kind of women they should allow backstage. I've always wondered how these random women hook up with rock stars, and now I know. They fit the description for the flavor of the night.

With all the chaos that comes with tearing down the stage and getting the talent tucked safely into their dressing rooms, I'm able to slip away undetected. Pushing against the flow of traffic sets my nerves on edge. I didn't expect to feel nervous about being away from Rhett. My heart races as bodies press against me. I find one of Rhett's men, whom I'd met earlier in the day, standing near the stairs leading into the lawn section of the amphitheater. I run to his side, thankful he recognizes me.

"Hey there, Ms. Lindsay. What can I do for you?" James asks with a bright smile. His easy demeanor sets me at ease.

"I was supposed to meet up with my friend, but I can't seem to find her. I left my phone in Rhett's truck and don't want to run all the way back down there to find it. Would you mind letting me use your phone really quick to call her?" I push all my nervousness aside and plaster a smile on my face I hope looks genuine.

James pulls his phone from his back pocket and hands it to me just before rushing forward to catch a drunk girl who tripped while she was walking—make that stumbling—down the stairs.

I take advantage of the distraction to gain some semblance of privacy while I call Tenille. She answers on the second ring.

"Bueno!" She always answers phone numbers she doesn't recognize with the Spanish greeting. It's her way of screening calls.

"Tenille." I almost choke on her name. Relief at hearing her voice overwhelms me. She brings me comfort when everything feels so uncertain.

"Lindsay? What's wrong? Where are you?" The concern in her voice is evident.

"Please tell me you're at the Shawn Cross concert tonight." There's so much noise around me, I can't tell if it's noisy on her end as well.

"Of course. Why do you ask?"

Shit, I hadn't thought about how I was going to explain my reason for being here after telling her I couldn't make it. I end up rambling the first thing that comes to mind.

"I made it after all and have a surprise for you."

"Oooh, did you find me a hot cowboy? I think I've got another round in me. Where are you?"

I glance at James. He's still preoccupied with the drunk girl, who is now sitting off to the side with an ice pack pressed to her forehead. She must have bumped her head on the railing during her fall. Thankfully, her mishap has kept James busy enough he hasn't been able to eavesdrop on my tall tale.

"I'm at the stairs on the east side leading up to the grass, but I can meet up with you wherever you are."

"Just stay put, and I'll come to you. I'm just walking out of the ladies' bathroom and it's a madhouse. We'll never find each other in this chaos. See you in a minute." With that, she hangs up. The timing couldn't be more perfect. James has turned the drunk girl over to a couple of medics.

I hand him back his phone and thank him as Tenille jumps on my back like the crazy person she is. I stumble forward before catching my balance, and she drops back to her feet. She links her arm with mine, shoots James a flirtatious wink, and drags me away.

I throw my arms around Tenille when she drops to her feet. I didn't realize how much I'd missed my friend while I was tucked away in a little lover's bubble with Rhett this week.

I've gone weeks without seeing her, but we text almost daily to check in, and everything is fine. I guess the threat of losing my life put things into a different perspective. I am going to make our friendship a bigger priority from this moment on.

"What the fuck, girl! You never hug me first. Everything okay?"

I squeeze her a little harder before turning her loose and stepping back. "No reason, let's go," I say, taking her hand and dragging her behind me.

"Does my surprise have anything to do with that nifty backstage pass around your neck?"

"Could be," I say, noncommittal. "By the way, what did you mean by 'got another round in me?' Were you fucking a stranger in the bathroom?"

"No, I was not fucking a stranger in the bathroom. I was fucking Ram in the bathroom," she says, pursing her lips.

I stop so abruptly, Tenille slams into me. "What do you mean you were fucking Ram in the bathroom? He's here?" My voice is shrill even to my own ears. My eyes frantically search the faces around us. I'm not sure who I'm looking for. I've never actually met Ram before. Tenille has always done a good job of keeping us apart, but that could all be about to change. He may be in a pseudo-relationship with Tenille, but his loyalty is to the MC. If he knows I'm here, I'm in deep shit.

"Somebody had to come with me since you backed out. He met me here, but he left when you called. Said he had club business." She shrugs like it's no big deal.

"Does he know I'm here?" I grab her shoulders and shake her manically.

"Why are you acting so crazy? No, he doesn't know you're here. He had to leave as soon as we finished. You called while I was washing my hands." She settles her fists on her hips.

I scrunch my nose in disgust and wipe my hand on my thigh.

She throws her hands up in annoyance. "I said I washed my hands! Stop acting like I gave you cooties."

"It's not cooties I'm worried about," I mutter.

When we arrive at the gate leading to the restricted area, the security guard tells me Rhett has been looking for me and wants me to meet him on the bus. Tenille's eyes grow huge.

The buses are parked in a basin-like area behind the stage. The road above is gridlocked with cars as the parking lot empties. Women lean out of their windows, screaming for Shawn's attention. Through the jarring sound, I hear the roar of several motorcycles fire up and their engines rev.

I freeze. My eyes dart around, trying to pinpoint their location. My eyes land on a group of bikers wearing the Zona MC cut. Blood pounds in my ears, my vision narrows, and I can't seem to catch my breath.

I watch as they weave around the cars, making their way out of the venue. When they get up onto the road, they ride single file down the middle stripe as though it's a lane carved out especially for them.

Terror seizes me as one guy makes solid eye contact with me and lifts his hand in a wave. They know I'm here. They know who I'm with. Why didn't they just take me out? Why only intimidate me like this?

I snap out of my stupor when Tenille punches me in the boob.

"Ow, what the fuck was that for?" I ask, rubbing the sting from the tender flesh.

"Look what you did to my arm!" Tenille exclaims, showing me the half-moon shapes indented on her forearm. In my panic, I grabbed her arm in a death grip. "What the fuck was all that about? You acted like you saw a ghost."

I stare at her, not knowing how to explain myself. I can't tell her about the threat against me. She'll freak out and call Ram to call off the dogs. She's so protective of me, she doesn't always see reason. In this case, it would hurt more than it would help.

"I'm sorry. I thought I saw an ex-inmate and didn't know how to act. I've never run into one on the streets before." I'm not a great actress, but I've been getting plenty of practice today.

She rolls her eyes. "You're so damn paranoid. They don't give a shit about you once they're released. Get over yourself. You deserve another tit punch."

Well, damn. I hadn't expected that. I mean, she's right. It seems arrogant to believe somebody would think about me when I'm no longer a part of their every day, especially for an ex-con. I'm sure I'm the last person they worry about once they're free.

I cross my arms protectively over my chest as Rhett approaches. His fingers tangle in my hair, and he presses a kiss to my temple. "I've got to go deal with some woman making a scene at the gate." He points at the entrance we came through. "Stay put, we need to talk about your little disappearing act."

I laugh at the comical way Tenille's mouth hangs open. Before she can ask about him, our eyes pull to a flurry of activity by the gate.

A very pregnant woman is yelling at one of Rhett's guys. She's on her

GREENLIGHT

tippy toes, leaning forward with her index finger less than an inch from his face. He looks down at her with a complacent expression. His lack of reaction is fueling her aggression.

"What seems to be the problem here?" Rhett asks in an authoritative voice.

The woman whirls around in a cloud of blonde hair and turns her attention to Rhett. I'm expecting her to continue her shouting, but instead, she collapses into Rhett's arms and sobs incoherently into his chest.

I'm momentarily stunned. The woman's volleying emotions give me a bit of whiplash. Just as I reanimate, Rhett leads the woman out of view of the public with his hand on the small of her back—like he did with me not so long ago.

Confusion takes hold as I slowly follow them, not entirely sure if I should or not. I don't know the protocol for handling an irate fan, but I can't imagine taking them backstage is the best way to handle it. This woman is unstable, and I could see her rushing Shawn if she caught sight of him. It wouldn't look good if the owner of the security company was the one who brought the threat straight to the target.

Who am I to second-guess Rhett's judgement?

When I catch up to them, they're standing beneath an overhead light against a block wall separating the backstage area from the public areas of the concert venue. The woman is propped up against the wall, while Rhett leans in close with his hand wrapped gently around her upper arm.

I'm almost there when I hear Rhett ask, "How far along are you, Amy?"

Amy.

The beautiful blonde pregnant woman is Rhett's ex, Amy. The woman who broke him so completely, when she prevented a pregnancy he thought they were trying for, is standing before him, telling him she's pregnant after all.

My world comes to a screeching halt. My stomach churns, there's a roaring in my ears, my chest is tight, and I'm desperately trying to draw air into my lungs. My vision narrows and blackens around the edges.

I have to get out of here. What the hell was I thinking, allowing myself to fall for a guy like Rhett? He's way out of my league. He's so good looking and muscular. Of course he's going to have a supermodel look-alike on his arm.

Even near the end of her pregnancy, she's stunning. She's taller than I am. Her hair is long and shiny and perfectly straight, unlike my drab brown, slightly frizzy locks.

Tenille must sense my anguish. She takes my hand and leads me through the thinning crowd toward her car. Tenille reads me well and is mercifully quiet while she begins our ninety-minute drive out of the city.

I know her silence won't last long. She'll demand answers of why I was at a concert I never should have been at. Why I'm so emotional and broody. Why I haven't answered any of the texts I'm sure she's been sending all week.

I'm granted about twenty minutes of solace while she navigates the insane amount of traffic created by over twenty thousand country music fans, all trying to get home at this late hour. As soon as she's merged onto the interstate, she turns off the radio and smacks the back of her hand against my shoulder.

"Talk," she demands.

I take a deep breath, releasing some of the tension in my body with a slow exhale. I've spent my small reprieve mulling over exactly how much of my situation to tell her. Some of it, I'm sure I'm bound to keep quiet about while it's being investigated. Other aspects, like certain dirty and intimate details, I want to keep for myself.

I've settled on the decision to share a CliffsNotes version of events. Some shit went down at work. They forced me to take some vacation time; it was strongly suggested I stay with a friend of a friend until it all blew over, things got a little hot and heavy, we went on a date to the concert, his old friend showed up, and she witnessed the rest.

I hope my watered-down story is enough for her to leave it alone. She's quiet for a few minutes, probably rolling my words around, deciding whether to let me get away with the vague truth.

No dice.

"I know you wouldn't lie to me. I believe every word of what you said, but I also know you left out a whole hell of a lot of details. I know your truck has sat in the lot at work since the day after you bailed on our lunch. You've not answered my texts or phone calls in all that time either. My guess is your phone is still in your truck. I don't know why you took off from work without saying a word to the only person who has your back. I know whatever happened with Mr. Friend-of-a-Friend was a lot more than a weird situation, otherwise you wouldn't be this upset. I'm sensing you're a little raw, so I'm going to let it go. For now."

And this is why she's my person. My best friend. My family. My only family, really. She gets me completely, unlike my actual family.

"Thank you," I say sincerely.

Tenille nods once, keeping her eyes on the dark stretch of desert highway.

With my forehead pressed against the cool glass of the window, the long day catches up to me, and I drift off into a light sleep for the rest of the drive.

I realize as she pulls her car into my driveway that my keys are in my duffle bag at Rhett's house. I can't even get in my house. I close my eyes, and my head thumps against the window. Here goes yet another lie to my best friend.

"I left my keys in the guy's truck. Do you have my spare house key with you?"

Tenille lets out an annoyed sigh and opens the console of her car. She lifts out a key attached to a key chain that says "best bitches." I have a matching one with her spare apartment key.

She gives me a sad smile. Pity paints her expression. She drops the key in my hand. "I'll be here at nine to take you to get your truck."

I nod and give her a half smile in thanks. I grip the handle and open the car door. When I have one foot on the ground, she calls my name and I turn back toward her. "I can tell whatever happened tonight has you shook, so I won't pester you. Just know I'm always here if you want to talk about it. I know I can be a bit of a bitch, but I love you, and I don't like seeing you like this."

I lean over and wrap my arms around her. She squeezes me tightly, and I hear a quiet sniffle. A lone tear sneaks out of my eye. No matter how annoying and abrasive Tenille can be, I wouldn't trade her for anything in this world.

I haven't ever been so grateful for her. Between her rescuing me tonight and the fear I felt when I thought the Zona MC was coming to kill me, I vow to never take her for granted again.

Before things can get any heavier, I jump from the car and slam the door. She doesn't pull away until she's certain I'm safely inside with the door locked. Tenille expresses love with little gestures like that. She rarely puts her affections into plain words—it's not her style—but I never question her love. She shows me often. I need to be better at reciprocating.

CHAPTER 13
RHETT

One by one, I talk to each of the men and women on my security team. Somebody had to have seen her walk out of the gate. I have four people set at each gate at the end of the night ensuring all concert goers peacefully make their way through the bottleneck created by the mass exit.

One of them saw her leave. They had to have. If not, somebody's getting fired. I don't care if it sounds unreasonable. I'm pissed she could walk away from me so easily. I'm pissed I was too distracted by my conniving ex to notice her leave until it was too late.

I wait at the time clock and ask each team member if they saw her as they leave. Everyone tells me the same thing: no.

I'm fuming mad by the time Jerry makes it to the time clock. I ask him the same thing I've asked everyone else, bracing myself for disappointment when he surprises me.

"Yeah, boss, she was talking to James during the final encore. She used his phone while he was taking care of a girl who fell and then she met up with some girl, and they walked back toward the concessions. I never saw her again after that. Is something wrong?" Jerry asks, concern clear on his face.

Biting the inside of my cheek, I roll his words around in my mind, trying to piece her actions together. She called somebody, a girl met up with her, and they walked away. She mentioned her best friend was a big fan of Shawn's.

Maybe that's who she called, and they left together. The last time I saw her, she was standing with a woman I didn't recognize.

A small amount of the pressure in my chest eases now that I know she's at least with somebody she reached out to and nobody took her. Then the knot ties back up when I ask myself why she left me.

I feel Jerry shift, trying to catch my eye, and I realize I never answered him. "All good, just a miscommunication is all." I try to manage a smile to set his mind at ease. It feels awkward and forced, and it's obvious he sees through my bullshit. Before he can call me on it, I ask, "I haven't seen James come to clock out. Do you know where he is?"

Jerry's brows draw in. "He went home about an hour ago. He called you on the radio and said his wife had called… something about one of the kids. You told him he was okay to head out."

Shit, how could I have forgotten? James is a cop by day, and he works for me to make a little extra money when he's unable to pick up overtime with the department. He and his wife were high school sweethearts, babies having babies, and he works himself to the bone trying to make sure she can stay home and raise their two kids.

"That's right. I forgot, with the unnecessary panic of not being able to find Lindsay. Thanks for the info and your work tonight," I say with a smack on his back. "See ya next weekend, Jerry."

We head in opposite directions, him to the staff parking lot and me toward Shawn's bus for the after party.

I don't feel much like partying without my girl, so I pull my phone out to call James and see if I can get the number Lindsay called. I need to know what happened.

Glancing at the screen before I unlock it, I realize it's well past midnight. James left at about 10:30 p.m., so he'd be home by now, taking care of his family and hopefully sleeping before his shift tomorrow. I can't call him tonight. I can't be that selfish. It'll have to wait until tomorrow. Tonight,

STEVIE LEE

I'm going to do my best to put this shit behind me. I'm going to drown my sorrows in whiskey.

Shawn wakes me the next morning, telling me the bus leaves within the hour to head to his next tour stop. My head is killing me, my mouth is dry and tastes like ass, and I need to piss like a racehorse. Maybe drinking the entire bottle was a bad idea.

I clean myself up in the bus bathroom, which is the size of a Cracker Jack box, using a spare toothbrush and some of the other toiletries these animals stashed for the girls they bed in every city.

I step out of the bathroom, and Shawn hands me two bottles of water, which I promptly down.

"You look like shit, bro. You all right to get yourself home?"

I nod mid-gulp as I finish the second bottle. "I should be okay now. I look worse than I feel. It was great to see you," I say as we go in for a hug. No bro hug this time. This is a full-on dick-bumping hug because he's my best friend and I probably won't get to see him again for a long time.

"Call me when you get home so I know you made it okay."

"Love you too, fucker."

As I drive through city streets toward the interstate, I call James and check on his kids. I'm desperate to ask for the phone number, but I'm not a total bastard. I care about my employees and their families.

He assures me the kids are fine, just one of those twenty-four-hour stomach bugs. Shit and puke are apparently everywhere, but they both woke up fine this morning.

"I know you care about my kids, but I also know it's not why you're calling. Jerry sent me a text warning me you'd be calling about the pretty brunette. She was good when she walked away with her friend. They were hanging all over each other like drunk chicks do, and smiling," James says to reassure me. "I'll text you the number she called so you can check on her yourself."

GREENLIGHT

I thank him and hang up, my fingers banging against the steering wheel with nervous impatience. He said they had seemed drunk, so now I'm worried one of them drove in that condition. Lindsay's not stupid. I know this in my heart, but my mind isn't being rational right now.

I'm this worked up and acting like a heartbroken fool over a woman I met only six days ago. I'm going to call and make sure she's okay and then I'm going to back off. If she wants me, she can track me down. She knows where I live, and she can get my phone number from Keith. I won't pursue another woman who doesn't want me like I did with Amy. I poured my heart and soul into that relationship, only to have my heart ripped out of my chest and stomped into the dirt. Never. Again.

The text comes through, and I take a deep breath before holding my finger on the number until the option to call it pops up. The ringing through the truck speakers breaks the silence. My heart pounds harder against the wall of my chest with each ring.

Pick up, pick up, pick up! Just before the call rings out, the line clicks.

"Bueno!"

What the fuck? "Uh, my… friend, Lindsay, called this number last night. I just want to check on her and make sure she got home safe."

"Well, well, well… If it isn't Mr. Magic Dick himself. How's the side bitch? All good, I hope. Not really. I don't give a shit. You just make sure you keep your heat-seeking-moisture-missile the hell away from my best friend! Whatever you've got going on with the hoochie should have been one hundred percent done and over with before bringing that fallopian fiddler near her.

"I've never seen her this upset over a man before. You must've got her dickmatized with that hymen hammer. I mean, I get it. I, myself, have been messed up by a good dicking, but this is ridiculous! She deserves better than to have some hot guy roll up with an enormous cock and use her like that. You should be ashamed of yourself!"

"I-I... Uh, what? What did she tell you? I don't understand." I stutter in disbelief. What the hell is this crazy woman talking about? What hoochie? What side bitch? And where in the world did she come up with all the names for my dick?

"All I know is she disappears with you for a week and calls me crying because she found out there's someone else in the picture. Now, I'm always up for sharing. The more the merrier, I say, but not my girl Lin. Nope, she's a straitlaced one-man-loving chica. I don't understand how you could limit yourself to one meat stick, but that's just her way. Anyway, motherfucker, I've gotta run. Don't call me again. Don't track her down. She's home. I'm taking care of her. She'll be fine as long as you don't fuck with her anymore." She hangs up abruptly.

I laugh out loud. I don't know what else to say or do. I don't know what just happened. That woman has a mouth on her worse than most of the men I served with in the corp.

I swipe my hand down my face, my palm scraping against my stubble, and shake my head with a mirthless chuckle.

My next call is to Keith. I have to know the status of the threat against Lindsay. If he tells me her life is still in danger, I'm hauling my ass down to her house whether she wants me there or not.

Keith picks up on the first ring. "Hey, man, I just got off the phone with Lindsay."

My heart rate picks up. "You did? Is she okay?"

"She's fine. She said she was ready to come home and face whatever comes her way," he explains. "She'll be returning to work on Monday."

"Is that really a good idea? She'll be walking into the lion's den." My foot pushes harder on the accelerator.

"She'll be fine. I'll make sure she has limited inmate contact. As for when she's not here, we're just going to have to trust she's strong enough to take care of herself." He laughs a little to himself. "If I had to bet on any of my officers being able to handle themselves, it would be Lindsay."

He's right. She's one tough lady. It doesn't mean I'm not still worried about her.

"Listen, Rhett," he says. "I probably shouldn't tell you this, but the Zona MC has bigger fish to fry. A rival gang got the jump on a couple of their members and killed one of them. Lindsay is the least of their worries right now."

"You're sure?"

"Yeah, man. I wouldn't let her come back if I thought she'd be marching to her death. Did something happen between the two of you?"

I suck in a breath. "I don't know, man. I feel like I need to work that out with her before I say anything. Just keep her safe for me. Can you do that?"

"Of course. I'm here if you need me, but try not to stress over this. She's going to be fine."

I hang up, feeling marginally better about Lindsay's safety. I don't feel any better about her being away from me though.

I'll leave her be for now. I'm hoping she comes to me, but if not, I'll go to her before too long.

CHAPTER 14
LINDSAY

I return to work Monday morning at my normal time of 8:00 a.m., looking forward to getting to the kennels to see Kody. Unfortunately, I'm stopped short by Payne the second I walk into the department.

"What are you doing here, Lanier? I thought you were supposed to report to shift on graves," he says with an apologetic look on his face.

I stare back at him with a confused expression. I don't understand. I thought they cleared me to return to my normal duties. I called Snyder when I got my phone charged. Since I wasn't officially on administrative leave—they basically tricked me into using my vacation time—he couldn't stop me from returning to work. When I don't respond, Payne continues.

"The email I got said you were going to be moved to night shift to be posted in Main Control for the foreseeable future. You're on PC status." He laughs like this is all a joke to him and not my life being affected.

PC status. Protective Custody.

They use that label for inmates who can't get along with the general prison population, child molesters, rapists, gang dropouts, rats… He lumped me in with them. I doubt it was his intention, but I can't help the sinking feeling in my stomach at the thought.

I finally find my voice. "So, you're telling me because I did my job better than you, I get pulled from a position I earned, put on the worst shift, and locked inside a control room on 'PC status' as you say. This is fucking ridiculous!" My voice rises with anger. "It's not enough this fucking place ripped me away from my life and sent me off with a stranger for a week. Now they're completely uprooting everything I've worked for. I didn't realize I'd be the one punished for finding the drugs I was supposed to find. What's next? Am I going to get fired too?"

Tears threaten to well behind my eyes. My nose burns a little. I refuse to cry. They won't be tears of sadness. No, they're tears of fury. No matter their source, they'll only be seen as weakness, and I refuse to look weak in front of this prick.

From the day I interviewed for my place within the K-9 department, I was judged and ridiculed by every man here. They all smirked and laughed at the "little lady trying to play with the big boys."

I showed them. I showed them I was more than capable of keeping up with every one of them, performing better than a few. I learned to be the best dog handler I could be and loved every minute. Kody is my partner, and together we've been unstoppable. We found more drugs in my year with K-9 than any other handler.

But apparently, that's the problem. We found too much. I didn't hold back. I let nothing slip by. I upset the status quo.

Prison gangs know their activity can't go undetected all the time, but it's worth the risk to get caught occasionally. When they get busted more often than they deem acceptable, they retaliate.

I fell victim to their retaliation when the Zona MC threatened my life.

The thing I've learned in the years I've been working here is not all inmates are bad people. Most are normal people who made a stupid mistake and are suffering the consequences of those choices. They aren't looking to hurt the staff and try to avoid conflict with other inmates when they can. They want to get through their sentence with the least amount of grief possible.

Feeling defeated, I head home, strip out of my uniform, and slip into a pair of tiny cotton shorts and a tank top. I have to report to work for a second time today in a little over twelve hours.

Disappointment consumes me. After devoting all my focus and energy, at the expense of my personal relationships, I lost the position I love. I developed feelings for Rhett and had the rug pulled from beneath me. And it appears I'm still not completely safe at work.

A girl can only handle so much. I'm going to handle my feelings today by sleeping. I tell myself it's because I work all night and need my rest, but really, it's because I can't face any of this right now.

I sink into my pillow, pull the covers up over my head, and shut out the world.

My tire is flat, its sidewall ripped open on the front driver's side. It wasn't like that when I came home this morning. It's not exactly something I'd miss and certainly not something that happened by accident.

My gaze roves over the surrounding area as I search for anything out of the ordinary. It's pretty rural out here, no streetlights, the only visibility coming from the glow of the single bulb on my front porch. I come up with nothing.

I don't have time to waste, and being out here leaves me feeling vulnerable. It's eerily silent, and chills snake down my spine at the thought that whoever did this to my truck could still be out here watching.

I quickly change my tire, keeping my uniform mostly clean. Thankfully, I'm heading in for my first graveyard shift. Nobody important will be there to judge the few dirt and grease stains marring my pants.

CHAPTER 14

LINDSAY

Main Control is a two-person, armed post. Since this room allows access to the outside, we are to defend it by any means necessary. Public safety is our top priority.

I internally groan when the second officer walks in a few minutes late.

Crane is a very… robust woman. But let me tell you, this woman has confidence in spades. She doesn't allow anybody to make her feel less than just because she isn't a size two. She might be plus-sized, but as she puts it, "Honey, there's just more surface area to love!"

Her size isn't what has me cringing to work with her though. I believe we should all be proud of the skin we're in. Love yourself, and all that.

My problem with Crane is her stories. She loves to talk to men online and then meet up with them to fuck. She refers to these men as "chubby chasers." It's apparently a kind of fetish she is more than happy to cater to, as long as the men in question have at least a nine-inch cock. She enjoys relaying these stories, in vivid detail, to anybody who will listen—and not necessarily willingly. Unfortunately, I'm about to be that somebody since I have nowhere else to go.

She's about to subject me to eight uninterrupted hours of graphic sexcapades. I may not have an issue with her weight, but it doesn't mean I want to continuously picture her in compromising positions.

GREENLIGHT

    I haven't worked in Main Control in over a year, but it doesn't take me long to get back into the swing of things. The routine is a little different on this shift, and I keep looking through the logbook at the previous night's entries to figure out what I need to be doing. There are inventories for equipment and keys that must be done. We also are the voice of the unit over the radio and intercom system.

    I volunteer to do the inventories and let Crane have the task of opening doors and gates while manning the radio. I need busy work to stay awake. Despite sleeping all night and most of the day, I'm feeling fatigued.

    I spend the first hour and a half of my shift with a clipboard, marking off the equipment. I check serial numbers on shotguns and Glocks against the inventory sheet and count the bullets before moving on to the lock box containing the inflammatory agents. Canisters of pepper spray line the shelves organized by type. The OC, made with natural irritants, in cans with orange writing is on the top shelf, and the OC/CS blends, made with natural and chemical irritants and marked with blue writing, line the bottom shelf. I nudge a can of OC over to count the canisters behind it and then subconsciously rub my nose. The citrusy scent of the gas causes it to tingle.

    I regret the simple action immediately when the skin around my nose and upper lip burns slightly, and the tingle turns into a violent sneezing attack. Fuck me, I know better than to touch my face when handling this shit. I can't even wash it off. Water seems to exacerbate the effects. I have to suck it up and let it wear off with time.

    I fan my face with the clipboard, the cool air helping to quell the burn marginally. Crane notices and throws her head back, laughing hysterically. I glare at her, which only makes her laugh harder.

    Ignoring my burning face, I begin the key inventory. Counting each individual key on each keyset takes the longest. The maintenance keysets have over thirty a piece, and there are five sets.

    When I'm finally done, my hands are black from God-knows-what and my stomach churns a bit. I'm not usually much of a germaphobe, but seeing the evidence of the filth on those keysets all over my hands is disgusting.

Thankfully, there's a restroom attached to the control room, so I'm able to wash the grime away before touching anything else.

Inventories have killed off the first two hours of my shift, leaving me with six more to get through. I sit back in front of my computer that controls the doors and gates for half of the facility. Crane helped me keep an eye on things and could control my side while I was busy most of the time. Occasionally, she'd let me know I needed to step over and open a gate when her side had more traffic than she could look away from.

"You want some?" Crane asks as she holds up a party-sized bag of Doritos. Was she planning to eat the entire bag herself when she packed it?

"Uh, no thanks. I'm good."

"If you change your mind, grab some. I don't mind sharing. Do you want something else? I've got a package of tuna, one of those really good frozen macaroni-and-cheese dinners... Let's see, what else is in here? Oh, a cup of soup, some crackers, because I gotta have crackers with my ramen. I think that's about it tonight." Crane looks up at me expectantly.

"No, really. Thanks though. My stomach isn't used to being up all night. I couldn't eat if I wanted to," I say apologetically.

She shrugs, letting me off the hook, and we work through the rest of the night—me in silence and her yammering on about things I pay little attention to. Luckily, she doesn't seem to expect me to comment back.

I'm exhausted as I gather my things at the end of my shift. I don't think I've ever looked forward to face-planting in my bed more than I am right now.

Along with my and Crane's relief comes the day shift sergeant. It isn't completely unusual for the supervisor to come up into Main Control, but something feels off with his presence today. He stands in front of the door, blocking my exit, and makes eye contact with me.

GREENLIGHT

"Lanier, I hate to do this to you, but I've got to ask you to stay and work an extra four hours in a housing unit," Sergeant Summers says with no hint of the remorse he claims to have.

I stand there, stunned. I've never been one to shy away from extra duties, always doing whatever's asked of me. But today, I'm so tired I want to stomp my foot and refuse to stay. My nose even tingles a little, like I might cry.

I suck in a deep breath, push down my exhausted toddler tantrum before it erupts, and nod my head. It's only four more hours. Plus, overtime means time and a half on my paycheck. Can't be mad about that.

Before I can ask for my assignment, Crane's cigarette-raspy voice breaks through my thoughts.

"I thought she couldn't have any inmate contact?"

Sergeant Summers shrugs his shoulders and looks unimpressed. "I don't know anything about that. All I know is I had a last-minute call-in and need somebody to fill in down in Baker Pod. We're so short staffed, I'm lucky to have one officer for each pod. Lanier is new to the unit and at the top of the list to be mandated, so she's stuck staying."

Crane looks from the sergeant to the two officers who have come to take our place and then at me before objecting once again.

"She's not supposed to have any inmate contact. If she has to stay, leave her in here and send one of these two out to Baker. I'm trying to save your ass right now."

The two day-shifters both make a disapproving sound. I really wish she'd keep her damn mouth shut. After eight hours in this damn box, the last thing I want is to do four more with an officer who isn't going to want to work with me if their partner gets booted from their post to accommodate me.

"Crane, it's fine. I'll work Baker. It's not a big deal."

"But—"

"It's fine!" I snap, cutting her off. "Give these guys their briefing so I can get Peterson off the clock. I'm sure he'd like to get home to his family."

Crane's lips press into a tight line. She's clearly not happy with the situation, but she nods anyway and has the good sense to not say anything else.

I make my way to the officer's desk in Baker to relieve Peterson and get a quick briefing of the goings-on of the block.

"Hey, Lanier! I thought you weren't supposed to be out here among the convicts. PC status and all that." Peterson laughs good-naturedly.

I smile a closed-lip smile and shrug. "I guess it doesn't matter when you're short staffed. Good of the facility and all that." I wink at my use of his words.

"Right, right. I get it. Well, there was a lot of tension brewing last night, but it was quiet after lockdown. Keep an eye out when they get let up for breakfast. I'm certain something is bound to pop off in the next day or so. They just need the right reason. One of the shot callers for the Zona MC got moved over here yesterday morning, and it's put everybody on edge."

That's not good, not good at all. The powers that be seem to think the threat against me isn't much of a threat anymore, but they've not completely let their guard down either by keeping me locked in a box with a side arm and a shotgun during my new regular night shift.

I work to keep my expression neutral and thank him for the heads-up.

I take my inventories and get my logbook entries caught up, readying myself for the first count of the shift. I'm thankful for this count taking place before breakfast. I'm going to get a chance to scope out the block while most of the inmates are still asleep.

I study the Baker roster, looking for a name that stands out as the ZMC's shot caller, but I come up empty. Either they recently promoted this guy up the ranks, or he's stayed off the radar. Neither scenario is good for me. I need to know who this guy is so I can watch him and who he associates with.

There's a good chance these guys are still pissed and want to kill me—

or at the very least, kick my ass.

Every member of the Zona MC has a specific tattoo somewhere on their body. The older members have theirs in more visible places. They wanted everybody to know who they were. They've since gotten wiser. The newer members are still branding themselves, but the tattoos are going onto more inconspicuous places so they can't easily be identified by prison officials and law enforcement.

If I'm lucky, this shot caller will be an older member with an obvious tattoo I might glimpse while I count each individual person. With a little more luck, he'll still be asleep and won't know I'm in the area.

I check every bed during my count and never come across the tattoo of the Arizona flag, tattered with ape hanger handlebars. Most are asleep and beneath their blankets. The few who are awake are dressed and sitting on their bunks, reading or drawing.

When I get to the cell where I'd found the picture of my truck, I notice he replaced it with one of a woman sharing an uncanny resemblance to me, holding the leash to a Belgian Malinois police dog. The MC is dropping subtle hints only I would catch to let me know they're watching. I'm going to be diligent and wary of every single person in orange. I'm not sure my tired mind can handle this level of concentration, but I don't have a choice. My well-being depends on keeping my eyes open and my suspicions raised.

Truthfully, it isn't only my well-being. If something pops off, every officer is at risk when they respond. And they would all respond. When an officer is in trouble, gray shirts come out of the woodwork. We always have each other's backs.

About fifteen minutes after Officer Griffin collects the paper I tallied my count on, Main Control announces count is cleared. That means the inmates' doors will open, and they'll be free to move around the dayroom and the rest of the unit. Breakfast will be served shortly. Any semblance of control I had over Baker Block just disintegrated.

My hands are a little sweaty, and my stomach is churning with nausea. I've never felt this level of anxiety within these gates. The slight fear I've always carried with me gives me an edge. It helps keep me sharp, but this overwhelming, all-consuming sense of dread is new. This is exactly what I felt when I watched those headlights come toward the cabin last week.

I focus on taking deep, even breaths while I jot the rest of the information in my logbook. I'm finishing up by adding my initials to the end of the line when I hear the whirring of the electronic locks cycling all around me. My illusion of safety is gone.

I sit at my desk with my radio clasped tightly in my hands and watch as every inmate in Baker Block makes their way to the growing line of the chow hall.

I only recognize a few people from my time before K-9. None of them make eye contact with me. Most don't even glance my way. These guys are masters of surveillance without making it obvious. I'm certain I'm being covertly cataloged. It won't be long before somebody comes up to ask me some nonsense question to scope me out a little more and report back to the shot caller. I know it for a fact.

My hope? They think I'm here for a full shift and take their time gathering their intel on me. I'll be out of here in just under three hours, and they'll have missed their chance to retaliate. Fingers crossed.

Breakfast passes smoothly. Nobody speaks to me at all, which is typical. Convicts don't get chummy with officers unless they're trying to manipulate us.

Once breakfast wraps up, the guys with jobs take off to their details, and a few others turn out for education classes. As I'm counting off the inmates going to the recreation yard, a young kid in a bright-orange uniform walks up to me.

"Hey CO, can I get a kyte?"

"You need to step back until I'm done turning out yard and then I can help you," I say assertively, never taking my attention off my task.

"Ah c'mon, CO, it'll only take a second. Just grab me a kyte really quick."

If I were a male officer, this is where I'd tell this guy to fuck right off, but seeing as I'm female, I can't get away with that. These guys won't tolerate being "disrespected" by a woman no matter the scenario.

I made the mistake of mouthing off after doing something a male officer had done right ahead of me, and I had an inmate try to put me in my place. Nobody around said anything in the moment, and I deescalated the situation and walked away unscathed, but later that night, they doled out a little prison justice in my honor.

I got lucky then. If something had happened during the initial encounter, I'd have been on my own until other officers could get to me. This time, I don't think I'll be so lucky. The MC wants me dead, and I can't give them an opportunity to strike.

I put my hand out, stopping the line, and make a mental note of the number already out on the yard before I turn to look the little punk directly in the eye.

"I told you to wait until I'm done turning out my yard. Now back off before I make your face match the color of your pretty new uniform," I say as I unsnap the holster for my can of OC, the only "weapon" provided to me by the department. I'm only granted less lethal means of protection on the yard since it would be much easier to overpower me and take my weapon.

His face turns red with a mix of embarrassment and anger, but he does as I've asked and walks away. He seems familiar, but I can't quite place him.

I continue my yard turn out, call my count in to Main Control, and make a note in my logbook. I've kept a visual on the punk from the corner of my eye the entire time, knowing he's probably the one sent to gather intel on me. As soon as I sit at my desk and pull the kyte from my drawer, he walks up and again demands I give him the slip of paper.

STEVIE LEE

I lose it. I know this is the worst time to lose my temper, but this little fucker isn't going to talk to me like I owe him any favors. He's all of eighteen years old, probably has only been locked up for a month or two. He's either stupid or this is his initiation for protection. Either way, I'm not tolerating his condescension today. I'm tired, and my patience is nonexistent.

"Listen here, you little fucker. I can tell you haven't been locked up very long, so let me break it down for you. You don't walk up to a CO and demand anything. You don't interrupt their duties, and you certainly don't talk to us with your little superiority complex. I can make your time here a living hell." I pause for a second, and a cocky smile overtakes his face.

"What are you going to do? Shake down my house? Go ahead, I need the trash to be taken out."

This time, I'm the one with the cocky smile. "Nope, I won't touch your house. I'm going to toss his." I point at inmate Hartley. "And make sure he knows you're the reason his house got trashed."

Jason Hartley is in his mid-thirties and has been in prison since he was twenty-two years old. He was working construction and had a disagreement with another guy on the crew. He tracked the guy down later that night and shot him in the chest with a shotgun at close range. Now he's serving life without parole. He's spent every day of the last fifteen years working out and turning his body into solid muscle. When he's not working out, he's adding tattoos. He is literally covered in them from the top of his head to his feet. He's an intimidating sight, for sure.

The kid visibly blanches as he takes in Hartley sitting a few feet away. Hartley looks at the kid menacingly before puckering his lips and kissing the air.

I laugh. "Hope your ass is ready for that pounding. Do they sell lube in the commissary?"

Hartley chuckles as the kid turns tail, rushes back to his cell, and pulls the door closed behind him. Hartley makes eye contact with me and nods once before turning his attention back to whatever it is he's doing.

If I can get through the next hour without any incidents, I'll be home-free and back to the safety of Main Control after my regular days off. I'm feeling pretty good. I haven't noticed anybody with blatant hostility toward me, and my little problem child has spent every minute since our altercation sitting on his bunk, doodling. He doesn't even spare me a glance when I walk by his cell on my security checks.

I'm walking back to my desk to make my logbook entry that everything is safe and secure. Nobody is dead or getting beat-up or raped and all is well, then it clicks. My problem child is the guy from the video Snyder showed me. He's the one who made it clear the ZMC wants me dead. The ID badge in his window said Jones.

Melody Jones... the woman Kody and I busted with drugs in her vag. That package was meant for him, and I gave him another reason to hate me. I humiliated him in front of another inmate. Shit.

I hear a loud, deep voice yell my name.

"Lanier!"

I turn around and see Hartley running toward me and a flash of bright orange coming up on my left. I spin fully to see that punk-ass kid, Jones, running for me with a shank raised.

Oh, fuck...

This is it. This is where I die. With a rusty homemade knife buried in my neck.

I grab the canister of gas off my hip and draw it forward to paint the little shit orange. I take a step back and spray in the general direction of his face as I sidestep. Unfortunately, it doesn't slow him down much. He continues to advance toward me.

I fall back on my training, striking the pressure point on his arm that forces his grip to release. The shank skitters across the floor, out of reach. Our bodies collide, my boots slip on the fallen pepper spray, and he knocks me off my feet.

Pain erupts when my body slams to the floor, and Jones lands a punishing blow to my face. The metallic taste of blood fills my mouth. I barely have time to get myself into a defensive position before Jones is over me, raining punches into my forearms. Drops of God knows what—saliva, snot, tears, sweat—mixed with OC land on my skin. It's the least of my worries as he pounds a fist into my ribs. I struggle to catch my breath while still trying to fend off my attacker.

Hartley slams into Jones, knocking him off me. I stumble to my feet, keying the mic on my radio to call for help.

The words barely leave my lips when Jones gets loose from Hartley and comes after me again. This time when Hartley tackles him, Jones grabs onto one of my legs, taking me down with them. The back of my head bounces off the concrete floor, and the air whooshes from my lungs.

My vision is blurry, and my head spins, but I can make out Hartley beating the ever-loving shit out of Jones.

From his perch on top of Jones, Hartley screams, "Get the fuck out of here!"

I drag myself up and lumber toward the door. It opens to a sea of gray rushing into the pod.

He came to my rescue. He defended me. A hardcore convict came to the aid of a correctional officer at the risk of retaliation from the other inmates, at the risk of picking up extra charges. That is my final thought before the lights go out and I lose consciousness, collapsing into the arms of another officer.

I come to in the health unit as I'm being loaded onto a gurney. I can't move my head, and panic takes over before Snyder's face appears in my line of sight.

"Lindsay, calm down. Your head bounced off the concrete, so they've put a cervical collar on you until they can be sure there isn't any damage to your neck. You're about to be loaded into an ambulance to be taken to the hospital."

His words don't really register, but the tone of his voice calms me. With sudden clarity, images of the fight rush through my mind.

I try to sit up while shouting, "That motherfucker tried to shank me!"

The EMTs shove me back down on the gurney. "You need to lie down and be still, ma'am."

I roll my eyes and instantly regret it as my stomach churns with nausea. I slam my lids closed and control my breathing, willing my stomach to calm. Each bump of the ambulance on the shitty Arizona roads all the way to the hospital causes my head to ache worse and worse.

Someone's fingers lightly drag across my forehead. A deep, masculine voice cuts through my aching, foggy brain. "I know you're in pain, but try to relax your face. The tension is going to make it worse." For a second, I think it's Rhett, and I blink my eyes open in search of his handsome face but only see Keith's concern. "Can't you guys give her something for the pain? She doesn't look well."

"No, sir, sorry. We want to make sure she doesn't have a brain bleed first," the EMT tells him.

"I'm fine, but it would be great if you could find a smoother road or a closer hospital. How much longer do I have to be strapped down in the back of this fucking box?"

Keith and the EMT chuckle at my expense. "We haven't even made it out of town yet, so you're looking at about another thirty minutes. Try to relax the best you can. Think you're up to answer a few questions about your medical history?"

"Sure," I reply, my eyes closed.

He rolls through a list of questions I answer the best I can without much thought. When he asks if there is a possibility of being pregnant, I squeak out a quick: "Maybe, but it's too early to know for sure."

Now I have an ache in my chest to match the ache in my head. I miss Rhett, even if it's only been a couple of days without him.

Keith coughs out a choking sound, and I realize I outed myself for sleeping with his friend. I groan out loud. "Damn it."

"Do you want me to call him to meet us at the hospital?" Keith asks with a touch of mirth.

I attempt to shake my head, but the collar prevents the movement, so I whisper, "Please don't. I'm not ready to face him yet." Tears pool in the corner of my eyes. Goddamn him for making me fall for him so quickly. I know he can't control that Amy showed up when she did or that she finally gave him what he wanted so badly. The timing sucks for me.

Mercifully, Keith leaves the subject alone and doesn't ask for an explanation to my comment. I know he's curious, and I can only imagine what scenarios he's got brewing in that head of his, but I have absolutely no plans to tell him anything.

We arrive at the hospital after what feels like the longest journey known to man on the most pothole-riddled road I've ever been on.

The doctor orders a CT scan first, and they draw blood to run a pregnancy test. The nurse tells me a blood test will be more accurate than a urine test this early.

I'm left to rest in my little sectioned-off space in the emergency room while we await the results of my tests. Keith has been by my side at every moment he could. He's not asked me about what happened between Rhett and me. He's been a silent and strong support system I needed much more than I care to admit.

We get the news I'm going to be fine in a few days. I made it through the attack with nothing more than a few bruises and a mild concussion. As I predicted, the pregnancy test came back negative, although the nurse reassured me not to give up hope because it's still too early in my cycle and there's still a chance. She gives Keith and me a sweet smile, like she's wishing us the best. It dawns on me she must think we're together. I'm about to protest, but Keith thanks her.

I look at him like he's crazy, and he winks at me with a little smirk. It's then the nurse tells him all of my discharge instructions. She ensures he knows how to take good care of me over the next few days while I rest and let my brain recover from the trauma of bouncing around in my skull when it smacked on the concrete.

Keith thanks the nurse for me again as she leads me through the doors and out to the parking lot. Shit, how the hell am I going to get home? Neither of us has a car, and once again, my phone is in my truck back at the facility. I'm going to have to ask to borrow somebody's phone to call Tenille, again, to come pick my ass up. She's going to fucking kill me if this headache doesn't do the job first.

I'm about to open my mouth to ask to use Keith's phone when a bright-green Jeep pulls up to the curb in front of us. I will never forget this Jeep as long as I live.

"What the fuck is Brandon doing here?" I ask before my mind can catch up with my mouth.

Keith's brows scrunch together in confusion. "How do you know what my son drives?"

The passenger door opens, distracting us, and Amber steps out with the biggest smile stretching across her face. She makes eye contact with me sitting in the wheelchair in front of her, and her smile drops as her eyes widen.

Brandon rounds the front of the Jeep and has an identical reaction. I can't help the laugh that escapes me. They are probably in a panic wondering what, if anything, I've told Keith about them.

"I asked Brandon to come pick us up so I can get you home and get my car from work. Is there somebody I can call to meet us there? You can't be alone for the next forty-eight hours."

"I'll be fine on my own. If you'll get me back to my truck, I can take it from there. I'll call my friend if I need anything."

"I'm not okay with that. Your discharge orders say you need someone to be with you for the next two days, and you need to be on total brain rest. You are certainly not driving yourself home from the facility. You either tell me who I can call or you're coming to my house until you're well enough to be on your own. Those are your only choices," Keith states matter-of-factly.

"What about Uncle Rhett? Why isn't he here, anyway?" Brandon might have been able to save himself from my earlier slip about me knowing him, but he killed all hope of that. Amber swings the back of her fist into his stomach to shut him up. Unfortunately, it's too little too late. Keith has caught on.

"All right, somebody needs to explain to me how Lindsay knew this is Brandon's Jeep and why you'd think Uncle Rhett would be here with her." Keith looks pointedly at Brandon, his arms crossed.

Brandon looks from me to Amber, back at me, and at the ground before finally making eye contact with his father. "Amber and I wanted a little time to ourselves, so we took a trip up to the cabin for a couple of days. I didn't know you had let Uncle Rhett and his girlfriend stay there, and we kind of crashed their party."

Keith huffs out an angry breath. "We'll talk about this when we get home," he says. Then he looks at me with clear curiosity on his face. Fortunately, he doesn't ask me about my relationship with Rhett and instead helps me up from the wheelchair and into the front seat of the Jeep.

Keith tells the kids to get into the back seat before turning back toward me. "Last chance. Tell me who to call to come stay with you, or you're coming home with me. You want me to call Rhett? There's obviously something going on there that neither of you have shared with me."

"There isn't anything to tell. We alleviated the boredom and then I was able to return to work and we went our separate ways. End of story. Give me your phone, and I'll call my friend Tenille. She'll come take care of me."

"I don't believe you, but it's not any of my business, so I'll leave it alone," Keith says as he hands me his phone.

CHAPTER 16
RHETT

I swallow repeatedly, trying to bring moisture back into my mouth while I stare at the Instagram photo my sister, Kelly, called me into the office to see. The image is of Lindsay's beautiful face, bruised and swollen. She posted a picture on Instagram a few days ago, tagging the ZMC's profile with the caption: "You can physically knock me down, but I will get up and come back stronger."

The muscle in my jaw ticks. I don't know if I'm more angry or guilty. Those rat bastards got to her. I should've never let her out of my sight. They wouldn't have been able to do this to her if I'd been there. I should've fucking been there.

"Rhett, you're scaring me. You're shaking, and your ears are bright red." My sister's whisper barely breaks through the noise in my head. I lift a trembling hand to my ear, and sure enough, it's hot as fire. I've never felt this much rage, not even after Amy admitted to being on birth control while I thought we were trying to conceive.

I shake myself from my rage-induced haze and punch Keith's contact info into my phone. I'm done waiting for her to come to me. I can't keep her safe if I'm not with her.

The line clicks and Keith says, "I wondered when I'd be hearing from you," by way of greeting.

GREENLIGHT

"What the fuck happened to her?" I growl.

Keith sighs heavily on the other end. "You know I can't tell you anything about an ongoing investigation or somebody's medical condition. What I can tell you is she's back to work, on graveyard, and her days off are Tuesdays and Wednesdays."

"I need her phone number."

"You know I can't give you that information either. Graveyard shift ends at oh six hundred hours. I wish I could tell you more than that, but I can't. Anything you'd like to share with me?"

"There's nothing to tell. You asked me to keep her safe, and I failed. I won't sit back and allow it to happen again." I can barely get the words out. My throat is still dry.

"Goddamn it, Rhett, you're baiting me to talk, and I can't. What happened to her had absolutely nothing to do with you. I'm the one who failed her. Don't start with this self-deprecating bullshit you like to pull when something happens out of your control. I've got a meeting to get to. I've given you all I can; it's up to you to figure out what to do with it." The line goes dead, and my grip tightens on my phone while I continue to stare at the image of my girl's battered face.

A notification dings on Kelly's computer, alerting us to a new image. She clicks on it before I have a chance to ask. I ball my hands into fists, trying to quell the shaking while the new picture loads.

When it finally pops up, I breathe a little easier. Lindsay's face looks a hell of a lot better. The bruising is more yellow than black, and the cut beneath her eye is nothing more than a faint pink line. She captioned this one: "You didn't scare me away. I'll be back tonight, fuckers."

My heart swells. I love how brave she is. She's never backed down. Even when she should've been scared shitless and cowering, she stood her ground. I'll never forget how she pulled herself out of her nerves at the cabin and focused on the threat. Even though it turned out not to be a threat at all, we didn't know that for what felt like hours. Most women would've collapsed in a heap of tears, but not my girl.

I've never met anybody like her. She's strong and fearless. She doesn't take shit from anybody, including me. I picked at her relentlessly, trying to keep her at a distance, but it didn't work. She fired right back, making herself even more attractive. I didn't make it an entire day before I succumbed to her charms.

I need her in my life. We may have only gotten a few days together, but it's all I needed to know she's it. They say when we know, we know. I never believed that until her. I think I knew it the moment I realized she kept a gun in her nightstand alongside her vibrator. She's a woman who knows what she wants. I just hope she still wants me.

CHAPTER 17
LINDSAY

Tenille has been checking in on me over the past week and took me to my follow-up doctor's appointment. After being off work for another seven days, I'm finally released from medical leave and can return with the promise I have no inmate contact and to take it easy. It means I'll have to stand up for myself and not allow my ignorant supervisors to post me anywhere other than Main Control.

I've settled into a routine with Crane. I do the inventories at the beginning and then she offers me food. Some days I accept; some days I can't stomach the choices.

I excuse myself to the restroom and scrub the grime from my hands. The smell of wet metal causes me to gag a bit. It's strange. I'm not sure why the smell is affecting me this way. I wonder if I'm coming down with something.

"Did I hear you puke?" Crane asks loudly as I step out of the bathroom. She has a large bag of Doritos sitting on the counter next to her. She shoves several into her mouth before turning to look my way.

Despite gagging moments ago, I home in on the chips. I don't normally eat a lot of junk food, but my mouth waters, and I can't stop staring at that red bag.

Crane notices. She's way too observant. I can already feel her scrutiny.

"Come on over and have a seat. I'll share my chips with you. You could stand to put a few pounds on. Men like a little extra cushion. You're too skinny."

I wholeheartedly take her up on her offer. I haven't been eating much since I've been home. My sadness has been a huge appetite suppressant. Just the thought of eating has had my stomach roiling. But these Doritos, they look better than a fucking Thanksgiving feast.

Walking out of the front gates into the parking lot, I enjoy the vivid colors of the sky as the sun rises. I take a deep breath of the fresh morning air, hoping it'll quell the nausea I've been fighting the past few days. I should have recovered from the concussion already, but I can't seem to shake the stomach upset.

Crane is prattling on about something, but I'm not really paying attention to her until she says, "Damn, girl! Which one of those two is the daddy to that baby?"

The fuck is she talking about?

When I look around the parking lot, I spot Investigator Kennedy walking my way with a shit-eating grin plastered to his face.

Shit. What the hell is he doing here? If he needed to interview me for the investigation, he would've come in during my shift, not catch me in the parking lot afterward.

Wait... Did she say two?

That's when I notice him leaned against the tailgate of my truck, looking all kinds of hot. I stop dead in my tracks. How am I supposed to deal with this right now?

I'm exhausted. I worked all night long. I've listened to Crane talk about all the men she's been meeting from the internet to fuck. It's probably been the source of my nausea. If I have to picture this woman one more time in compromising positions, I might puke in her lap.

Crane's obnoxious laughter pulls me back to reality. "Girl, good luck there. I think I might sit and watch the drama unfold while I smoke a cigarette."

"Oh, fuck off, Crane. I'm not pregnant, so neither of them is my baby daddy."

"Girl, if you're not pregnant, then I'm not fat!" She cackles as she climbs into her car.

By then, Kennedy is standing right in front of me with a confused look on his face. "Hi, Lindsay. I haven't heard from you since the investigation wrapped up and thought maybe I could take you out for breakfast this morning. You know, since we've never gone on a date and all. Maybe after everything, you might've changed your mind."

My eyes dart from Kennedy toward Rhett, standing ten yards away with his arms folded across his chest. Kennedy glances over his shoulder to see what I'm looking at.

When we look back at each other, disappointment's written all over his face.

"So, I'm guessing he's the baby daddy?" His lips tighten into a thin line, and he looks down at his feet.

"Ugh, no! I'm not pregnant. But since he is here, I can't go to breakfast with you this morning. He and I should probably talk."

"No worries. Is there another day that works better for you?" Kennedy asks, hopeful. Before I can tell him I'm not interested in ever going out with him, a menacing voice interrupts.

"Sorry, buddy, she's not available," Rhett says gruffly as he comes up to stand beside me.

I'm getting a headache to go along with the nausea. I rub my hands against my face, stopping to massage the tension out of my temples. The testosterone swirling between the two men might be hot to witness on any

151

other occasion, but right now, all I want is to shower off the stink of the prison, crawl into my bed, and sleep for the next twelve hours.

I take a deep breath and heave out an exasperated sigh. "Look, guys, I can't do this right now. I'm tired and not feeling very well, so I'm going to go home."

Without acknowledging Rhett, I walk to my truck, open the back door on the driver's side, and unsnap the keepers from my duty belt. I don't even know why I'm still wearing the fucking thing every night. I don't have a use for it working Main Control.

"Will you please stop ignoring me, Linds? We really need to talk about whatever happened at Shawn's show. Why did you run off? What did I do? And what the fuck is that lady talking about? Are you pregnant? I deserve to know if you're carrying my baby. I can't believe you didn't tell me!" Rhett's voice is a little shaky, likely with nerves and emotion.

I rest my forehead against the frame of my truck, refusing to turn around and look at him. I need to hang onto my anger and hurt so I don't fall back into his arms. If Amy is having his baby, I'm not going to get involved with that nightmare, but I know if I look at him right now, I won't be able to resist him.

If I'm being honest… I've missed him. A whole fucking lot.

"Please, Lindsay, I need some answers. I've been going crazy for weeks now. I can't take it any longer. If you don't want me, that's fine, but at least give me the courtesy of telling me what I did wrong. And please, please don't keep that baby from me," he whispers.

I finally gather enough courage to look at him, and he looks wrecked. The lines around his eyes and across his forehead are drawn tight. He's right; he deserves answers.

"Rhett, I'm not pregnant. I'm not keeping anything from you. Right now, I'm tired and I don't feel well. Can we talk about all of this later tonight? I really need to get some sleep and then maybe I'll be up to talking to you before I come back to work tonight."

He shakes his head. "We don't have to talk right this second, but I can't sit around all fucking day waiting for answers. I'll follow you home and we can talk there. I won't keep you long. I need to know what happened."

"Fine, but I'm taking a shower before I do anything else." I step back to shut the back door, and Rhett opens the front door for me and waits for me to climb up into the seat.

Once I'm settled, he leans in and, with a hand to the back of my head, presses a kiss to my temple. I close my eyes against the tears springing unwanted to my eyes. I've missed those sweet kisses so much. I put the key in the ignition and fire up my truck.

"I'll see you in a few minutes."

I don't wait for Rhett to follow me into the house. I head inside and sit on the bench by the door to remove my boots. Leaning over to unlace them, my nausea rears its ugly head with a vengeance.

I run for the bathroom with my hand clamped over my mouth. I make it just in time before another round hits.

I lay my head on the toilet seat, panting. Tears streak down my cheeks from the effort of heaving. A damp washcloth suddenly drapes over the back of my neck, and a cool water bottle is pressed into my hand.

I open my eyes and find Rhett standing above me.

"Where the hell did you come from?" I ask him irritably.

"When I was walking up, I saw you running through the window and thought something might be wrong. I walked through the front door in time to see you drop to your knees in front of the toilet." He sits on the floor and leans his back against the cabinet. "How long have you been throwing up?"

"I don't know, a few days… a week. I've got some crackers and ginger ale in the kitchen. I'll start feeling better soon. Thank you for this," I say, lifting the washcloth from my neck and wiping my mouth with it. I take another sip of the water and let the cool liquid soothe my throat, which is raw from the acid.

"Are you still maintaining you aren't pregnant?" He raises his eyebrows questioningly.

Jesus Christ! Why does everybody keep saying that? I'd like to stay blissfully unaware for as long as I can. After all, the test at the hospital was negative.

It's pretty fucking obvious I'm pregnant, but I'm fine living in denial for a little while longer.

"Fuck off, I'm not pregnant." I say, rolling my eyes. Fuck, I shouldn't have done that. It does nothing for my headache still building behind my eyes. I scoot from in front of the toilet to rest my back against the bathtub so I can face Rhett.

"Sweetheart, you can keep denying it all you want, but it won't make it any less true. We fucked, unprotected, several times while you were ovulating, and now, you're puking your guts up. Have you bothered to take a test?"

He reaches out and takes my right foot into his lap. I never got my boots off before I got sick, so he finishes pulling the laces loose and tugs my boot and sock off. I quickly draw my foot back, worried about it being sweaty after more than eight hours confined in leather. Just as quickly, he grabs my ankle to keep my foot in his lap and shoots me a look like "don't even think about it," then pulls my left foot over to repeat the process.

"Yes, they did a blood test at the hospital last week, and it was negative," I tell him defiantly.

"All right. So you've had your period since we were together?"

I shoot him a scathing look. He sure has no qualms asking personal questions, but I guess I already knew that. I sit quietly for a moment, looking him over. It's been several weeks since I've seen him. He looks so good. I can't believe I walked away from him. His eyes look tired. They've lost a little of the spark they had during our time together, like he's been stressing about something. Maybe he has. Maybe he's stressed about having a baby with a woman who broke his heart. Not me, his ex. He's probably not thought about me at all.

He's here demanding answers from me, but he hasn't bothered to give me any information, so I think I'm going to deflect and turn this interrogation onto him.

"When is Amy due?"

"Amy? I don't give a shit about when she's due. I want to know when you're due and why you've been suffering through all this morning sickness alone. If you wouldn't have run away from me, or at the very least told me you weren't feeling well, I would have been here for you every day. Tell me why you ran."

Damn it. How did he turn this back around to me so quickly? I take a deep breath, closing my eyes, and try to calm my nerves. It's difficult admitting my jealousy got the better of me. I'm also confused now as to why he'd not be concerned about his other child. I get that Amy hurt him irreparably, but I know he wanted a baby with her, and now that there's one on the way, I can't imagine he'd turn his back on his own child, no matter who the mother was.

"I don't understand. Why don't you want to know when your baby is going to be born?"

"Of course I want to know. Why else would I be here? You disappeared, and I couldn't get Keith to give me your phone number, so I decided the only way I was going to get answers was to show up. I haven't stopped thinking about you. I was sick with worry, wondering where you went. I spent the rest of the night looking for you. I missed half the after party with Shawn because I was questioning all the guys on my team, trying to find out if any of them saw you leave. It wasn't until the next morning when I called a guy who had gone home early, and he told me you used his phone to call a friend for a ride home. I tried calling the number, but I got a lady who bitched me out for calling her."

I can't help but laugh. Tenille didn't tell me he had called her, but it doesn't surprise me she talked some shit to him after seeing how upset I'd been. I kind of feel bad he missed spending time with his cousin though. I know they don't get a lot of time together and try to make the most out of what little of time they can carve out of Shawn's crazy touring schedule.

I owe Rhett an explanation so I explain it all, about seeing him comforting a very pregnant Amy and concluding she must've gotten pregnant right before they broke up and was just now telling him. I told him I panicked. I thought he'd drop me and take her back since they had history and now had the future he'd dreamed of.

"I ran because it was easier to walk away before you kicked me to the curb. Before you could hurt me." I sniffle and realize I have a tear running down my cheek. Why the fuck does this make me cry? I said he didn't hurt me, so there shouldn't be any tears. Ugh, hormones! Not pregnancy hormones, the PMS kind of course. Nope, not pregnancy ones.

I chance a look at him, and his lips purse, and his forehead wrinkles in thought. After we stare into each other's eyes for a few seconds, his features soften in understanding and relief.

"All of this time apart and anguish was for nothing. Amy's baby isn't mine. She's been out of my life for over a year."

My heart sinks. I threw away all this time with Rhett because I let my emotions get the best of me.

"Some guy she was casually dating knocked her up and then bailed. She's panicking about being a single mom, and she thought she could come crawling back to me and I'd step up and play daddy to her baby. I sent her packing. If she could avoid getting pregnant with me for so long, she should have been able to prevent it after me too. Her mistake isn't my responsibility. Plus, I wasn't going to get involved with her when I had you."

"But you didn't have me. You told me we were just casual and to wait and see what happened. I thought I was making it easy on you by taking myself out of the equation. Not that I thought you'd even considered choosing me over her. She's really pretty." I whisper the last line. I look down at my hands in my lap, picking at my dry cuticles.

Rhett stands and grabs my hands, then hauls me to my feet. He wraps his arms around my shoulders and pulls me in tight against his chest. He lays his cheek on the top of my head and says, "Lindsay, you are who I want. I had Amy, and she wrecked me. Any attraction toward her is long gone. You are beautiful. I can't wait to watch your belly grow round with my baby."

These damn not-pregnancy hormones are at it again. This time, they've got me full-on ugly-crying into Rhett's chest.

He pulls the pins from my hair, releasing the bun and allowing it to fall in long waves down my back. His magic fingers massage the tension from my scalp, much in the same way he did the first night in the cabin. I melt into him. God, he's so fucking perfect. And I wasted the last month not being with him because I ran before I had all the answers. I'm so fucking stupid.

"Come on, let's get you into the shower. After that, I'll lie down with you and you can get some sleep. We'll talk some more after you've gotten some rest."

I nod and turn my head up toward his face in anticipation of a kiss.

His face stays expressionless, and he doesn't lean in toward me. I'm starting to feel hurt. I thought we were okay now. Then I realize I've got barf breath. I wouldn't want to kiss me either. I laugh and turn away from him to head down the hall toward the master bathroom to get ready for a shower.

I stand in the shower, brushing my teeth and letting the water soothe away my headache and the tension in my body. I've found, recently, it's easier to brush my teeth in the shower. My gag reflex has been more sensitive between the foamy toothpaste and scrubbing near my throat. If I'm going to puke, I'd rather do it in the shower than the sink.

Movement in the doorway grabs my attention. Rhett leans on the frame, watching me.

"Mind if I join you?" he asks, pulling his shirt over his head.

I don't respond. I watch with rapt attention as he sheds the rest of his clothing and steps into the shower with me.

Rhett takes his time washing me from head to toe. It's sweet and sensual. I'm too tired for it to be sexy, and Rhett seems to understand without me telling him. God, he's so perfect.

He dries our bodies and leads me to my bed. We lie naked under the sheet, facing each other. He tucks a strand of my hair behind my ear and leans in to kiss me sweetly.

"Come here, baby. Get some sleep." He pulls me against him, wrapping his arms around me, making me feel safe.

These last few weeks without him have been lonely. It's funny... I spent years alone and never felt lonely. A few nights with Rhett and I've forgotten what it's like to be content on my own.

I kiss his pec, right above his heart, and drift into a deep sleep for the first time in weeks.

RHETT

Fucking finally. She's in my arms, and everything is feeling right in my world again.

It's like she ripped my heart from my chest and took it with her when she walked away from me last month. I've been dragging myself through my days, being a shadow of a person, irritable and angry.

When Amy showed up, my world tilted. I knew it wasn't my baby in her belly—that wasn't what got to me. It was the fact the bitch would work so hard to ensure she didn't get pregnant while I thought we were actively trying to, only to turn around and accidentally get herself knocked up by some random guy. I felt oddly relieved.

If she could be this crooked, I was thankful we'd never had a child together and she was no longer a part of my life. I dodged a bullet.

Amy thought I was so desperate to become a father I'd take her back with open arms and pretend she hadn't betrayed me, that I would be so excited at the idea of having a kid with her, I would pretend it was mine.

Maybe I could have if I hadn't met Lindsay. At one point in my life, I loved Amy and thought she was it for me. Her baby is going to need a father, but it isn't going to be me.

I am hoping Lindsay is pregnant.

It's crazy to be excited about the prospect of having a kid with a woman I've only spent a week with, but I can't help it. There's something between us I can't ignore.

I tried. I tried to play it casual. I even told her to just have fun and not read into anything, but I think I was saying those things more to myself than to her. I was already gone by then, past the point of no return, as they say. I knew I wanted to be with her, but I was terrified she'd hurt me, like Amy did. If only I could stay detached emotionally, I could protect myself.

That worked out so well before. I don't think I kept up the façade for an hour before I poured my heart out to her at that little dining room table.

I search through Lindsay's cabinets and refrigerator but find she's apparently been living off of water, ginger ale, and oyster crackers, whatever the fuck those are.

She's dead-to-the-world asleep, so I slip out to make a run to the grocery store to get some food so I can make her breakfast when she wakes, and I'm going to get a pregnancy test.

She can't live in denial anymore. We both need a definitive answer and then we need to have a heart-to-heart and plan for our future. Because we are going to have a future. I've known it since the moment she climbed into my truck. I think she's known too, but she won't admit it to me or herself.

I put the test on the sink in her bathroom after I put the groceries away, so she can't miss it when she gets up.

She literally hasn't moved an inch in the hour I've been up. She looks beautiful and peaceful, despite the shadows beneath her eyes.

I feel awful she's been tired and sick for weeks without support from anybody else. She got stuck on the graveyard shift and has clearly struggled to adjust to the hours with everything else piled on top of her. That's going to change. I won't let her do this alone.

As far as I'm concerned, she can quit her job and take it easy for the rest of her pregnancy. I can't help but worry about her after the incident she was involved in right after she returned. It's one more thing we need to talk about.

As I finish up Lindsay's breakfast, the front door opens, and a woman's voice rings out. "Hey, bitch! That sexy black Dodge is parked on your street. We should sit out on your porch and wait to see what house he comes out of. Maybe you can see him this time!"

I laugh. Apparently, Lindsay and her friend have talked about my truck at some point. She can't see me in the kitchen from the front door, but I hear her pause whatever it is she's doing when I laugh.

The woman steps around the corner with a curious look on her face. "Why the fuck are you here, and where is Lindsay?"

"You must be Tenille. I'm Rhett. Lindsay is still in bed, although you probably woke her up with all your yelling about my truck." I offer her my hand for a handshake.

She stares at me for a few seconds, sizing me up, before she steps forward and shakes my hand. "All right, Rhett, now that I've embarrassed myself, how about you tell me what you're doing cooking breakfast in my best friend's kitchen at two o'clock in the afternoon?"

I laugh again. She's a feisty one, for sure. I'm not sure what Lindsay has told her friend about us, if anything at all. It doesn't seem like she's told her a whole lot, considering she didn't know who I was when she walked in the door, so I probably shouldn't divulge too much.

"I'm just visiting."

Tenille arches her eyebrow at me. "Uh-huh. Well, I'm going to go check on my girl." She hooks her thumb in the direction of the hallway before spinning around and walking away.

This could get interesting.

CHAPTER 18
LINDSAY

I wake up to the shrill shrieking of none other than Tenille. My stomach is a little queasy, but the urge to vomit is less than it has been on most mornings. My bladder, however, is another story.

I walk into my bathroom to take care of business first, grabbing a T-shirt and a pair of cotton shorts on my way. On my counter, I find a little white stick waiting for me.

Suddenly, I remember the events of the early morning hours with Rhett. He must have gone out and bought a pregnancy test while I slept. I guess I can't avoid the truth any longer.

After peeing on the absorbent part of the stick, I cap it and set it back on the counter, refusing to look at it until the full recommended three minutes pass.

While washing my hands, I feel Tenille's presence.

"What the fuck is this? Are you pregnant? You let him fuck you bare? You hardly know him. Why haven't you told me about it? And why is that guy out there? He's the black truck guy! I knew he looked familiar at the concert." Tenille's barrage of questions has me rolling my eyes as I walk out of the bathroom and sink back into bed. I am not ready to face her interrogation.

"Everything all right?" Rhett's deep voice fills the room, and I feel a little twinge in my chest. I could get used to hearing his voice every morning—or I guess afternoon, technically. But it's morning to me, so I'm going with that.

"No, everything is not all right. She took a fucking pregnancy test!" Tenille's voice is grating on my nerves. If she doesn't stop soon, I'm going to have to search for a roll of duct tape to put over her mouth. And I mean the whole roll, wrapped repeatedly around her head.

"You took it? What did it say?"

I roll my head back and forth across the pillow. "I don't know. I haven't looked at it yet. It's on the counter." I point lazily toward the bathroom.

"So wait… You've been fucking him, and you might be knocked up? You go, girl! No, I mean, why the fuck did you not tell me about this?" Tenille smacks my leg.

I don't answer her. Rhett disappeared into the bathroom and has been eerily quiet.

I rise from my bed and step around Tenille to see Rhett standing with his back toward me. He's holding the pregnancy test in front of him, staring at the results. After a moment, one hand drops to the counter and the other grips the bridge of his nose at the inner corners of his eyes, and he tips his head back to look toward the ceiling.

He's overcome with emotion, but I can't tell if he's saddened or happy.

I wrap my arms around his waist and lay my head against his shoulder blade. I hold tight, hoping to bring him comfort if it's what he needs. For me, I want to feel connected to him as I find out if I'm going to be a mother soon.

More of Tenille's incessant rambling comes from behind me, demanding answers.

"Tenille! Can you give us a minute? I'll explain everything to you soon." I don't care if I hurt her feelings. This right here doesn't concern her. This is between me and the man I'm potentially going to be linked to for the rest of my life, despite only having spent a few days with him.

Rhett's hand settles on my arms against his belly, and he rubs small circles on my skin with his thumb.

Once I know for sure Tenille has left the room, I ask, "Well, are we going to be parents?"

I barely have the words out before Rhett spins around in my arms, wraps his arms around my torso, and picks me clean off the floor. My arms and legs automatically wrap around him, and my face buries in his neck. I hold on, letting his warmth sink into me, and his woodsy scent fills my lungs.

"Is it completely crazy that I think I'm in love with you?"

I laugh and draw back so I can look into his eyes. "I'm guessing the test was positive and you're happy about it?"

"I'm very happy about it," he says without hesitation and kisses me soundly.

When we break the kiss, he carries me to the bed, crawls overtop of me, and kisses my neck. I tilt my head back, giving him further access. I must've moaned out loud because Tenille's voice echoing throughout the house breaks the moment.

"All right, I gave y'all motherfuckers a minute to get yourselves together, not to fuck while I wait ever so patiently to find out what the fuck is going on!"

"I guess we'd better go talk to her. We've got a lot to talk about ourselves, and the sooner she has answers, the sooner she can leave," Rhett says.

"Hey, mister! She's my best friend, and if you're going to be a part of my life, you're going to have to get used to her being around too."

"Whoa, whoa, whoa! Calm down, sweetheart. I didn't mean anything by it other than we could use some privacy to sort out where we go from here. That's all."

The softness in his eyes makes mine prick with tears. My pregnancy hormones have my mood all over the place. One second, I'm ready to rip his balls off, and the next, I want to cuddle and kiss him.

I'm owning the pregnancy hormones now. I think this might work out rather conveniently after all. Either way, it's going to be a long nine months.

RHETT

I don't think I've ever felt this happy in my entire life. I've got the girl of my dreams holding my hand, leading me out to her living room to tell her best friend she's pregnant with my baby.

She's pregnant. With my baby. I'm going to be a father.

Fucking finally!

We sit on the couch across from Tenille, who is propped up in a chair and glaring at us.

"Spill it, bitch. You've been holding out on me for far too long."

Goddamn, Tenille is a firecracker.

I resist telling her to watch the way she's talking to Lindsay. I don't want to get my head bit off again for insulting her friend.

Lindsay pulls her feet up beneath her and settles against my side. I reach over and take her hand, lacing our fingers together, and rest our joined hands in my lap.

These last few weeks have been hell without her. The almost-week we spent together, she got so fucking deep under my skin. I've been a mess since she walked away from me. I can't explain it.

I wouldn't say I believe in love at first sight, but it almost feels that way with Lindsay.

My mom once told me love isn't always an emotion. Sometimes it's a decision. There are going to be times in a relationship when the emotional love is going to fade into annoyance, or anger, or hurt, or any other number of emotions. In those moments, love becomes a decision. You decide to love them through all the shit.

She put it much more eloquently.

The moment I saw those two pink lines on the pregnancy test, I decided to love her. It doesn't matter if we can't make a romantic relationship work. She is giving me something I have wanted more than anything. She's going to be the mother of my child. For that reason alone, I will love her for the rest of my life.

"So, how big is lover boy's dick?"

Wait, what? Did Tenille just ask about the size of my cock?

"Tenille, you seriously did not ask me that in front of him!" Lindsay laughs. I guess she did.

Tenille shrugs and purses her lips. She turns her gaze toward me, smiles, and says, "Since she won't tell me, why don't you show me?"

My jaw hits the floor. I swear it. I've met some forward women, but this girl takes the cake. I don't even know how to respond. With my eyes bugged out of my head, I look to Lindsay for some help.

She isn't any. Help, that is. She's completely doubled over in laughter, clutching our linked hands to her stomach.

"Oh, my God! Tenille, you can't ask him that!"

"I'm just curious. I figure if he's able to pull you out of your ridiculously long dry spell, he must have a magic cock. And since I'm a bit of a cock connoisseur, I want to see all the cocks. So can I see it?"

I rub my hand down my face and hold it over my mouth, muffling the "Jesus Christ" I can't contain. "I'm going to use your bathroom."

I rise from the couch and stretch my arms above my head. My T-shirt rises and bares a strip of my six-pack. Lindsay's gaze lowers, and she drags her teeth against her bottom lip. I smile. I love that I affect her this way.

As I stand in front of the toilet, dick in hand, the door suddenly flies open. I turn my head, expecting to see Lindsay standing in the doorway, although I'm not sure why she'd feel the need to come into the bathroom while I'm taking a piss. Instead, I'm met with a gawking Tenille.

As I tuck myself back into my pants, her eyes trail up toward my face. "So are you a grower or a show-er?" she asks without any hint of shame.

"Excuse me?"

"Goddamn it, Tenille! Did you walk in on Rhett trying to catch a glimpse of his dick?" Lindsay yells from down the hall.

I can't help but laugh. I'm not insecure, so I'm not bothered that she's seen my dick. I wouldn't have whipped it out to show it off. That's kind of skeevy, although Tenille walking in here like this is probably skeevier. I laugh again. This shit is unreal.

"I'm just saying, if he's a show-er, that's pretty impressive, but if he's a grower... Do y'all have any interest in a threesome?" Tenille shows a slight amount of humility for the first time, in the form of a blush staining her cheeks.

I step up to Lindsay and take the offered bottle of water, then take her face in my free hand and kiss her gently. Tenille's "aww" makes me chuckle. I can't believe this hot mess of a girl is going to be a prominent part of my life as my girl's best friend.

I stand on Lindsay's front porch, watching her say her good-byes to Tenille. They hug for a long moment, murmuring words I can't hear.

As Tenille's taillights disappear down the road, Lindsay wraps her arms around my waist and lays her head on my chest. I hold her to me and bury my nose in her hair, breathing in her sweet scent.

She backs away, lacing our fingers together, and leads me back inside, straight to her bedroom.

Our lips collide. Her fingers sneak under the hem of my shirt to trace the ridges of my abs.

I take control of our kiss, slowing down the frenzy. As much as I've missed being inside of her, I don't want this time together to be like this. I want to take it slow and show her what she means to me.

"Are you sure you're up for this? We don't have to mess around if you're not feeling well."

"I'm sure. I want you," she says, dragging my face back down to hers.

We continue to kiss and caress as we make our way to the bed, only breaking apart long enough to pull our shirts off.

I lay her down and step back. My eyes trace every inch of her body. My fingers hook into the waistband of her tiny shorts, and I slowly drag them down her legs.

"No panties?" I quirk a brow at her.

She shakes her head, drawing her lips between her teeth in a coy smile.

I'm glad I didn't know before; I wouldn't have been able to focus on anything else.

I kiss my way up one leg, then the other. I drag my lips along her pussy, not lingering or applying any of the pressure she craves. The scent of her arousal fills my nose.

I plant a solid kiss on her stomach beneath her belly button, where our child is beginning to grow. My eyes lock with hers; my hands knead her full breasts. They feel larger and heavier already.

A breathy noise escapes her lips when I suck her nipple into my mouth, my thumb circling the other. My cock aches to be inside her, but I'm not in a hurry. I'll get there.

Lindsay's nails rake along my shoulders, not enough to break the skin but enough to send currents through my entire body.

I rise from the bed to my full height. Her eyes watch as I unbutton my jeans and lower the zipper. I shove them to the floor, along with my black boxer briefs. My cock springs free, bouncing against my stomach.

She stares at my hard cock and licks her lips before sinking her teeth into her bottom lip.

I grin, loving the effect I have on her. "See something you like, sugar?"

"Mm-hmm." She reaches her hand out toward me.

I lace our fingers together as I climb on top of her. I pin her hand to the mattress next to her head, cupping the back of her neck with the other. I kiss her slow and deep, and her hips lift to meet my body.

Her free hand trails down my side, causing goose bumps to erupt. She grabs hold of my cock and guides the head into her.

I lift so I can watch as I disappear inside her. Her fingertips bite hard into my ass cheeks, trying to pull me into her faster, harder. I don't give in. I continue my gradual pace until I'm fully inside. I push forward, nudging deeper before sliding almost all the way out.

With each thrust, I grind my hips into her, putting pressure and friction on her clit. A breathy moan meets my ears each time. Her body trembles as her climax nears.

My neck heats, and my balls tighten. Pressure builds at the base of my cock, so I slow my movements, trying to keep my orgasm at bay long enough for Lindsay to get hers. I keep my strokes short, ensuring constant contact with her clit.

"Rhett!" she screams as her body pulses, lighting my nerves on fire. Her orgasm spurs my own, and I release inside her.

Our bodies are drenched in sweat, our chests heaving with labored breaths. Our kisses are sloppy with the loss of control.

I wrap my arms around her back, holding her to me. With our foreheads together and our breathing rhythmic, we come down, stealing soft kisses between breaths.

CHAPTER 19
LINDSAY

We lie in bed after cleaning up from our lovemaking. I always thought the term "making love" was cheesy, but it's exactly what we did. It was slow and tender compared to the feverish fucking from before.

I feel more connected to Rhett, emotionally. Like our souls magnetized and attached to one another the second he settled inside me. I thought the feeling would subside afterward. Maybe I was feeling all the things because I was in a cloud of lust, but the haze has dissipated, and I still feel it. Deeply.

We lie snuggled up, him on his back, me on my side with my head settled into the crook of his shoulder, my knee across his thighs. He runs his fingers through my hair soothingly. My fingers twist and pull the hair running beneath his belly button. The room is dim as evening approaches. I have to leave for work in a few hours.

We're quiet for a long moment, each of us lost in our own thoughts. When I asked Rhett at the cabin what we were doing, he told me to keep it casual and let things play out. Things have played out, all right, but what does it mean for us now?

We're going to have a child together, so our lives will always connect. The chemistry between us is undeniable, but is it enough?

Rhett's chest vibrates as he says, "I can practically hear the wheels turning in that head of yours. Out with it."

I debate what I want to say. Do I lay my cards on the table, or is it too soon?

"At the cabin, you didn't want to put a label on things. Do you still feel that way?" I decide to keep it simple, let him lead this conversation. His answer will tell me whether I need to shutter my feelings.

His muscles tense, and his fingers stop running through my hair. He draws a deep breath into his lungs, my head lifting as his chest swells. He slowly exhales through his nose, and his breath flutters small pieces of hair across my face, tickling my cheek.

"I told you to keep things casual because I was trying to protect myself. I knew my feelings for you weren't rational, and I was afraid if I came on too strong, you'd push me away. Not only that but your life had just been flipped upside down. I knew you had a lot to process and there was a lot of unknown to your future. It wasn't the time to start something serious. I told myself if you and I were meant to be more, we would get there eventually."

My heart races, and my eyes sting with the threat of tears. These hormones have turned me into a crybaby. I don't like it.

When he doesn't continue, I nudge him in the ribs. "You didn't answer my question."

He sighs. "I hoped you wouldn't notice. I'm ready to do whatever you want. We can move at whatever pace you're comfortable with. I'm not going anywhere. I'm all in."

I roll onto my stomach and prop myself on my elbows so I can look directly into his eyes when I say, "Me too."

His smile stretches across his face. He grabs me around the waist and spins us so I'm beneath him. His fingers dig into my sides, tickling me. I giggle like a little girl and writhe to escape his grip, my hands shoving at his chest. It's like pushing against a wall, unmovable.

He grabs hold of my wrists and pins them to the bed. His face softens, his eyes locked on mine. "I want you to meet my family."

My eyes grow wide. I don't think I'm ready. He looks so hopeful; I can't hurt him just because I'm a chickenshit. I nod with a small smile. "Okay. When?"

"When are your days off? I'll set up a barbecue at the house." His face lights up with excitement. The corners of his lips lift. I can do this for him.

"I work two more nights and then I'll have the next two off. How big is your family?" I ask apprehensively.

"Just my brother and his wife and son, my sister, and my parents. You okay with that?"

I nod. It shouldn't be too overwhelming. *I can do this for him*, I repeat to myself.

CHAPTER 20
LINDSAY

Our tangled fingers rest on the console between us while Rhett drives toward his house.

The past two mornings, he's been waiting in my driveway when I get home from work. He takes care of me while I fight through the morning sickness and then he holds me until I fall asleep. When I wake, my house is clean, laundry done, and breakfast waiting for me. He's a better housewife than I would be.

The thought draws my lips up into a beaming smile. I could get used to Rhett taking care of me this way. I wouldn't have ever admitted it, even a few months ago. I prided myself on being independent, but a few days of not having to face everything alone has changed my feminist attitude. I can still be a strong woman, able to take care of myself, yet lean on a man for support. He's been treating me as his equal, never less.

I stare across the cab of the truck at his handsome face, his strong jaw highlighted by the setting sun behind him. Behind his sunglasses, the creases at the corners of his eyes deepen, and he glances back and forth from the road ahead to the rearview mirror. His knuckles whiten as he grips the steering wheel tighter.

Something is wrong. He leans forward, getting a closer look at his side mirror. The muscle in his jaw jumps.

"What's going on?" I ask. My nerves build from his obvious unease.

"There's two motorcycles a couple cars back. The headlight on one keeps catching my mirror when he pops into the lane. He's had several opportunities to pass and hasn't taken them. I think they're following us and letting me know they're there," he says through gritted teeth.

I glance through the back window and see two guys riding side-by-side wearing black leather vests. The only identifying marks I can see are a ZMC patch on one shoulder and a 1 percent on the other. I twist back around in my seat. My hands shake, and my stomach churns. My chest grows tight. When is this shit going to end? How much more of this can I take?

"They're definitely ZMC. What do we do?" My voice comes out a shaky whisper.

Rhett squeezes my hand. "Breathe, baby. If they were going to do something, they wouldn't make it so obvious they're following us. Keep your eyes out for any other bikes and try to relax. We're almost to the house. Use my phone to call Trent and put it on speaker. I'm going to have him open the gate so we can pull straight in."

As we slide through the gate to Rhett's property, the bikers cruise right on by, each with a middle finger raised high. I exhale a heavy breath as the gate closes behind us.

When Rhett's truck stops in front of the house, I notice three other vehicles that weren't here when I visited before. His family is already here. I can't believe I didn't connect the dots when we called his brother to open the gate. I should've, but my mind couldn't see past the panic.

Rhett watches me like I'm about to bolt. Truth is, I might. How am I supposed to plaster on a smile and face a house full of people for the first time? I can't possibly make a good impression on them while my mind is racing with fear-riddled thoughts.

My tears well, and my chin quivers with an exhale. Noticing my turmoil, Rhett flips up the console between us and drags me to his chest. He holds the back of my head as I cry into his shoulder. He kisses the top of my head and rubs my back, the action soothing my frayed nerves.

The passenger door is wrenched open, and an enthusiastic voice fills the cab of the truck. "Where's this girl my boy is so excited for me to meet? Oh…" Her voice drifts off when she catches sight of my sobbing form.

"Give us a minute, Ma?" Rhett mumbles.

"Okay, sweetheart. We'll be inside," she says sweetly before closing the door.

I pull myself together, dabbing tears from my face. The bruising from my attack is almost gone, just a slight yellow hue on my cheekbone surrounding the pink raised mark where the skin had split. I was able to mostly hide it with a little makeup. My efforts were probably all for nothing now that I've cried.

"Shit," I murmur, looking at my makeup-stained fingers.

Rhett rubs my fingers on his pants. "Don't worry about it. You look beautiful."

I snort out an unladylike laugh. "How am I supposed to explain my fucked-up face to your family? They're going to be thrilled to find out their son is dating a woman with a fucking target on her back."

"Stop it," he says harshly. "Your face isn't fucked up. If anybody even notices, they're not rude enough to say anything. Now, let's go in there and have some dinner. Don't worry, they're going to love you."

He helps me down from his truck, and we walk hand-in-hand toward the house. When we reach the bottom of the stairs, I stop him. "Are we going to tell them about the baby?"

He bounces his head back and forth in thought. "What do you think? Do you want to tell them now or wait? I think it's normal to keep it to ourselves until you're three months along."

I like the sound of that. I know they aren't stupid and will be able to do the math in three months and know I got myself knocked up right away, but

GREENLIGHT

I'm willing to put off their judgement for as long as possible.

"Let's wait," I say.

Dinner went surprisingly well. Rhett's twenty-one-year-old sister, Kelly, is sweet but maybe a little naïve. I can tell her daddy and big brothers have kept her sheltered from the big bad world. She works for Rhett, doing the administrative side of his business. She still lives at home but chattered on and on about moving in with her girlfriends when the new semester starts. She's majoring in business.

Rhett's older brother, Trent, is kind of scary. He didn't talk much, and when he did, his words were brusque. He and his wife weren't affectionate with one another and only spoke when it came to their son, Lawson. I tried not to judge their lack of affection; I understand not all couples engage in PDA, but it's hard to understand when I can't imagine not touching Rhett in some small way every chance I get.

Lawson was adorable, with blond wavy hair and piercing-blue eyes like his daddy. He was full of energy and had his grandparents, aunt, and uncle wrapped around his little finger. They catered to his every whim, even when he was perfectly capable of doing things for himself. He kept dropping his napkin on the floor and asking his Uncle Rhett to pick it up. Every time, he'd grin mischievously at me while his hulking uncle crouched under the table to do his bidding.

Watching the two of them together warmed my heart. It gave me a small glimpse into what Rhett might be like as a father to our child. It was sexy. I completely understand the term DILF now. He is a daddy I definitely would like to fuck.

Rhett's dad, John, is stoic but friendly. He sat at the head of the table, smiling with pride at his children and grandson. He talked little, seemingly happy to watch everyone else.

I'm rinsing and drying dishes as his mom, Charlotte, washes. "I'm sorry about interrupting earlier. I hope you're all right."

I struggle to keep my face neutral. I was terrible at lying to my mom as a kid, and this feels the same as I stand in front of Rhett's mom. What am I supposed to tell her? *Oh, everything's fine. No need to worry. We were followed here by two crazy motorcycle gang members who want to kill me. You know, everyday kind of things.*

Somehow, I don't think that's the best answer. I also can't tell her I'm overly emotional from the new pregnancy hormones invading my body.

She must sense my indecision because she pipes up with another question. "When are you due, sweetheart?" Her eyebrows raise, and she's got an enormous smile on her face.

This question catches me even more off-guard than the first. She pulls me into a hug, suds still clinging to her hands.

"You don't have to hide it from me. A mama knows these things. Now, I know y'all are new, but we don't have to worry about that. I'm so happy to have another grandbaby on the way. How far along are you?" Her excitement is a relief. I want his family to accept me, and I knew winning over his mom and sister was going to be the hardest. I think I'm one of the lucky few, granted immediate acceptance.

I shrug. "I don't know how far along I am. I found out for certain a few days ago, but I was living in denial a little longer than that."

"Well, if my son's behavior is any indication, I'm guessing you're probably about six weeks along. He was sure grumpy a week ago, but his attitude completely turned around several days ago," she says.

Rhett's and Trent's voices rise from out on the porch off the kitchen. It's tough to make out what they're saying, but I have a strong feeling it's about me.

"Trent is protective of his family. I'm sure he's worried Rhett's jumping into things too quickly." Charlotte gives me a sympathetic look and leads me away, so I don't have to witness Rhett fighting with his brother over me. I hadn't expected he would be the one to disapprove of me.

When we reach the living room, Trent's wife, Rachel, is getting Lawson rounded up to go home. She sees me walk in and gives me the same look Charlotte did. "Don't worry about him. He's got a stick up his ass about everything lately. Their fighting isn't truly against you. He'll come around eventually." She takes Lawson's hand and walks out the front door. Her car starts up a moment later, its headlights illuminating the boys. She backs up before Trent realizes Rachel is leaving him behind and jogs over to jump in the car.

Rhett's sister and parents leave moments later, with a much nicer parting than Trent and Rachel. I collapse onto the couch, relieved I got all of that out of the way.

CHAPTER 21
LINDSAY

After two months together, Rhett and I have settled into a nice routine. He stays with me during my work week, and we spend my days off at his house. When it works out, I go with him to concerts. I haven't spent a minute alone since we reunited. I'm with Rhett or I'm at work, still in Main Control.

I thought I would get sick of being in someone else's company constantly after spending so many years on my own, but I've come to appreciate the companionship and comfort Rhett brings. I feel safe when he's around, which isn't easy these days.

Butch has made it his mission to intimidate me whenever he can, and when he isn't available, he has one of his men do it. They walk by the bar-covered plexiglass windows, making sure they have my attention. Once they know I see them, their behavior varies. Sometimes they stare me down. Other times, they flip me off or throw some crude gesture. Whatever it may be, the message is always the same. *We see you.*

When I get in my truck at the end of my shift, I'm surprised to find a text from Rhett waiting for me.

Rhett: I'm running late this morning. Drive straight home and lock the doors. Call me once you're inside, so I know you're safe. Keep your eyes open.

GREENLIGHT

Something doesn't feel right. Rhett is never late. He's annoyingly early most of the time. I debate calling him to find out what's going on, but it's probably better if I do what he says and get my ass home. If I'm on the phone with him, he'll distract me, and I won't pay as much attention to my surroundings.

My fingers cramp from gripping the steering wheel too tightly. I'm trying to fight back nerves. I'm so tired of living in constant fear. I had hoped once I stopped finding their drugs, the Zona MC would forget about me. No such luck.

I don't know if this will ever end. I could get a different job, but what if it still isn't enough for them? They may not be satisfied until I'm dead.

My eyes scan in every direction as I pull into my driveway. Everything looks normal. It's calm and quiet this early in the morning.

There's a cigarette butt at the bottom of my porch stairs, but it's not strange. That's where Tenille sits to smoke when she's here, and it might be from her, even if I haven't noticed it before.

Inside my house, nothing seems out of place as I flip the deadbolt. I check the lock on the back door to be safe before calling Rhett on my way to the bedroom. He picks up before the first ring even finishes.

"Hey, sugar, you make it home safe? I'm sorry I'm not there yet."

"All good here. Everything okay with you? You're never late," I say as I step through the door. I gasp and stop dead in my tracks. My hand flies to my chest as though it could calm the race of my heart.

My underwear drawer has been pulled all the way out of my dresser, and my panties have been flung around the room. A frilly thong I never wear hangs from the light fixture. There's lipstick graffiti on the mirror hanging over the dresser.

We're coming for you Lindsay Bitch.

The phone drops from my hand as I bolt for the bathroom. I make it as far as the sink before the contents of my stomach make an appearance. I've still been nauseated most mornings, but I haven't vomited in over a week. This must be from the overwhelming fear consuming me.

They've been in my house. They've been in my fucking house.

I sink down and scream in anguish until my throat feels raw. I sit and stare at the floor, breathing rapidly while tears stream down my face. The only thing I can hear is the blood pounding in my ears. I close my eyes, fighting the dizziness.

For all I know, they could still be here waiting for me. I can't bring myself to worry about that. Death seems like a welcome reprieve to the constant state of fear I've been in for months. My sense of peace and serenity is gone, seeming never to return.

My hands settle on the tiny bump where my baby is growing. My tears come faster, blurring my vision. I'm not ready to die. I want to meet this perfect baby Rhett and I created, but what kind of life can I give him or her if there's an ever-present threat looming?

RHETT

Lindsay's gasp into the phone, followed by silence, has my heart in my stomach and a knot in my throat. I yell her name, but the only answer is a thud when her phone must hit the hardwood floor.

I curse under my breath. I can't believe this shit. I intended to leave with plenty of time to get to her house before she did, but when I went to leave, my truck wouldn't start. I found one of the fuel lines had vibrated loose. It only took me a few minutes to fix it, but it took me at least fifteen minutes to find the problem.

The fitting to the fuel pump must have vibrated loose, so I tightened it back up. It seemed unlikely but possible. Now I'm wondering if they did this, to keep me from Lindsay this morning. I hadn't considered our routine could put her at risk. It didn't matter if they were watching because she wasn't ever supposed to be alone. I'd always be there to protect her.

I underestimated them. My lack of judgement left her vulnerable, and it's my fault she's in trouble right now.

I downshift and push the pedal to the floor. Black smoke billows from the exhaust. I have to get to her as fast as I can. My mind races with the possibilities. They're kidnapping her and will be long gone by the time I get there. They're raping her. Or beating her. They've stabbed or shot her.

"Goddamn it!" I scream at the top of my lungs. How could I let this happen?

When I pull up to Lindsay's, I don't bother parking nicely on the curb. Instead, I cut the wheel and bounce to a stop in the middle of her front yard. I stomp my foot on the parking brake and rip my keys from the ignition.

As soon as I step out of my truck, Lindsay's piercing wails meet my ears. My mind conjures images of her being raped by those sick fucks. I sprint to her door and somehow get the key in the lock with the tremor of my hands. The second the lock clicks open, I slam the door into the wall and tear through the house toward the sound of Lindsay's tortured cries.

I barely register the mess in her bedroom when I discover her bawling on the bathroom floor. The stench of vomit permeates the air in the confined space. I fall to my knees, taking her face in my hands. My thumbs frantically brush tears falling in a continuous stream down her cheeks.

"Lindsay, baby, are you hurt?" I force the words through the lump in my throat.

She closes her eyes and takes a deep, shuddering breath. "No," she rasps out.

Relief washes over me as I rest my forehead against hers. I don't know what I would've done if I'd walked into one of the scenarios I pictured. Scratch that. I know exactly what I would've done. I'd have beaten them to death with my bare hands. Then I would have hunted down every member of that fucking gang until I'd slaughtered them all.

"What happened? You scared the shit out of me," I ask her, my tone gruffer than I intend.

She clears her throat and winces. Her throat must be raw from the combination of crying and puking. "When I walked in here, I noticed my panties thrown all over the place and the message on the mirror." She takes a deep breath that shudders on the way out, her chin trembling. "I panicked. Rhett, I can't live like this anymore," she cries.

I pull her into my lap and shift enough so I can survey her bedroom while I comfort her. Truthfully, the damage is minimal. Put a drawer back in her dresser, put her underwear away, and wash the mirror and nobody would ever know anything was amiss. Everything this club has done to show her the greenlight is still active has been subtle and not necessarily violent, but the stakes keep getting higher. The social media posts. A flat tire. Following us to my house. Piles of cigarette butts across the street from her house. Little things to let us know they're still around.

This escalation has me more than nervous. They violated her space this time. This is more personal and intentional. I'm afraid if we don't stop this or get completely away from it, the next time won't be so painless.

I'm tossing the underwear in a trash bag while Lindsay showers. She said she couldn't bring herself to wear them again after some creep had touched them. I don't blame her.

I got the sink full of puke unclogged without filling it up more with my own. Barely. Lindsay was mortified, but I'll happily clean up her regurgitated dinner over not having her here with me.

We talked about notifying the police but decided against the idea. The ZMC has several from the local force on their payroll, and while she could

GREENLIGHT

report it to that douche Kennedy, she felt like he wouldn't take her seriously anyway after our parking lot confrontation.

I convinced her to spend the day at my house. I had my sister check my security cameras to see if anybody had tampered with my truck. The feed was clear. My messed-up fuel lines were an unfortunate fluke. I feel safer having her locked in my house, on my gated property with a security system. She has nothing more than a cheap deadbolt on her house, which didn't keep her house secure.

I pack a bag with a few of her things I think she'll need to get by for a few days. If there's anything I missed, I'll buy it for her.

When I get her tucked in to sleep for the day, I go downstairs, intending to call Tenille. I saved her number after I called her when Lindsay left me, in case I ever needed it again. I'm so glad I had the forethought.

"Bueno," she says when she picks up.

"Tenille, it's Rhett. I need to talk to you about something."

She shrieks in my ear. "Is there something wrong with Lindsay or the baby?"

"No, no, she and the baby are fine. I know you're with one of the members from the Zona MC. What do you know about the greenlight they have on Lindsay?" I ask, trying to keep any accusation out of my voice. I don't understand their friendship. I can't see why either of them would be friends with the other when I consider their backgrounds, but I trust Lindsay's judgement.

I suspect their friendship has been rather convenient to the ZMC. She could be feeding them information on Lindsay. She could have supplied them with her house key. It would explain why there was no sign of forced entry. I grit my teeth at the thought. I hope I'm wrong, for Lindsay's sake. She couldn't take the heartbreak right now.

"I don't know anything about a greenlight. Is that why she freaked out at the concert when she saw Ram ride off with his crew?"

"They were at the concert too? Fuck, I didn't know." I scrub my hand down my face in frustration. "Tenille, listen. Lindsay had a major drug bust a couple months ago, and your guys threatened to kill her. They've been leaving a trail of threats ever since. They broke into her house last night and trashed her bedroom. She's scared shitless. I don't know how much more she can take. Do you think you can talk to them and get them to leave her alone? They've kicked her out of K-9, so she won't be stopping any more of their drugs from coming into the prison," I say, pleading with her.

Sniffles come through the line. "I didn't know any of that. She told me she was having problems at work, but I didn't know it was related to the guys. I'll talk to Ram and see what I can find out. He keeps me away from club business, so I'm not sure if he'll tell me anything, but I'll try. I can't believe he'd do this to me. He promised not to mess with her."

"Thanks, Tenille."

"Keep her safe for me, Mr. Magic Dick. I love that girl like a sister."

"You have my word. Take care of yourself. If they give you problems for asking questions, get the fuck out of there and call me. I'll get you both away from this mess if that's what it takes."

"I will. I'll call you when I know something."

Three hours later, she calls me back. The Zona MC wants to meet with me. Still worried about leaving Lindsay by herself, I schedule the meeting during a time when my sister will be working at the house. She can monitor my security system and make sure this isn't a setup to get Lindsay away from me so they can make their move. I told Lindsay Trent needed help with a construction job for my alibi.

I pull into the parking lot of the bar where Tenille works. She crosses the parking lot and meets me before I can even climb down.

"If you have a gun on you, leave it in the truck. They're going to pat you down." She stares up at me, hands on her hips.

"You're crazy if you think I'm going in there unarmed."

"No, you're crazy if you think they're going to let you in there with a gun." She shakes her head in irritation. "Trust me on this, Rhett. They won't hurt you unless you give them a reason to. Don't be an asshole and get yourself killed."

I nod in agreement and unbuckle my belt to remove the holster with my Glock.

"Nice, I get to see the goods again," she says, eying my zipper.

"You're too damn much, Tenille." I slide my gun under the seat and lock my truck. With a long exhale, I clap my hands together. "All right, let's get this over with."

I settle my hand between Tenille's shoulder blades and follow her through the massive wooden door. It's dimly lit inside, and there's a smokey haze in the air. Somehow, I'm going to have to sneak into the shower and wash my clothes before Lindsay's hypersensitive nose picks up the smell of cigarettes.

The door has barely closed behind us when a big guy stops me with a hand to my chest. "Turn around and put your arms out," he tells me in a gravelly voice. I do as he says and accept the pat-down, wincing when he smacks my balls and slides his hands down my pant legs.

"Really, Paul? Was it necessary to ball-check the guy? I told you he wouldn't be armed when he came in," Tenille says.

Paul laughs. This guy's a dick.

Paul leads me to a table and points at where he wants me to sit. He takes the chair to my left. The man across from me has the vice president patch on his leather vest. He eyes me speculatively.

The man sitting to my right smacks Tenille on the ass. My hackles rise. I hate seeing women treated like that. "Hey, dollface, grab Rusty and Paul another drink before you head on upstairs."

"You got it, Ram," she says with a tight smile.

So this is Ram. I'm not sure what Tenille sees in him. He's older than me by quite a few years. He's a big guy but looks like he's sporting more fat than muscle.

Rusty takes a swig of his beer, sizing me up. He turns in his chair, making sure Tenille has left the room before speaking. "So you're here to save your little girlfriend, is that right?"

I clear my throat, my nerves choking me. "We just found out she's pregnant. What's it going to take to put an end to all of this? You've scared the shit out of her. She's lost her position in K-9, so she's not even a threat to you anymore."

"Because of her, we lost an awful lot of money. We need to be paid," Rusty says.

"With interest," says Paul.

"How much are we talking?" I ask. Could this really be as easy as throwing a little money their way?

The three men glance around the table at each other before their gazes settle on me. "Fifty thousand cash and she quits her job. We don't want to see her anywhere near us again."

Fuck, I don't have that kind of money lying around. I rub my hand against my mouth while I contemplate what to do. "I don't have access to that much money. I think I can convince her to quit, but is it really necessary? Like I said, she isn't with K-9 anymore."

"Fifty grand and she quits, or we kill her and you too." A menacing smile takes over Rusty's face. "Or she can come work her debt off. I bet we've got a few clients with a pregnancy fetish."

Bile creeps up my throat, and the color drains from my face. They'll have to fucking kill me before I let them anywhere near Lindsay. "I'll come up with the cash, but I'm going to need a few days."

"You've got two days. You'll give the money to Tenille, and she'll deliver it to us. Lindsay doesn't step foot in the prison ever again. That's not negotiable. Make it happen, and we'll leave her alone."

GREENLIGHT

I'm going to have to move some money around, but I can get enough together if it means Lindsay and the baby are safe. If I can't convince her to quit her job, I'll get Keith to fire her. I hate the idea of forcing her away from her career, but I hate the idea of her being dead more.

"All right, consider it done." I stand from the table and reach out to shake their hands. Rusty looks at my hand, then back up at my face before returning the gesture. I hope their word and handshake means as much to them as it does to me.

As I pull open the door, a man shouts, "Forty-eight hours or you're both dead."

I don't acknowledge him. They'll get their fucking money, and I'll get to keep my family intact.

I stalk across the parking lot, the gravel crunching under my boots loud in my ears. I have enough money in savings, but I'll have basically nothing left. I hate the idea of not having my savings to fall back on, especially with a baby on the way. I'll have to see about cashing in on some of my investments to replenish my account. It's worth it to be done with this shit.

A hand grabs my arm, ripping me from my thoughts. I spin around with my hand balled into a fist. Tenille cowers, and I drop my hand.

"I didn't mean to startle you. I was calling your name, but it was like you couldn't hear me," she says timidly.

"I'm sorry. I was stuck in my head, trying to figure out how I'm going to come up with fifty grand in cash in two days without Lindsay noticing. Hop in, we need to talk."

She glances over her shoulder as if checking to see if we're being watched. "I've got to open the bar in an hour."

"I'll bring you back before then. We need to get our story straight. I don't want Lindsay to know about this, and I'd rather not talk about it here."

She nods her understanding and walks around to the passenger's side. It's comical to watch her climb up into the cab with short legs. When she's finally settled in her seat, she flips me off for laughing at her.

A mile down the road, the tension slowly eases from my shoulders, and I feel like I can breathe again.

"Let's tell Lindsay I got Ram to convince the club to leave her alone as a favor to me. It's not a complete lie. I got him to arrange this meeting. She doesn't need to know the rest. Please tell me you have the money."

"I've got the money. It's going to pretty much clean me out, but I've got it," I say confidently.

Tenille stays quiet for a minute, staring out the window. "Rhett, I've got to get away from them too. It makes me sick they were willing to kill my best friend over some fucking drugs."

I didn't see that coming. I don't really know how to help her. I can't offer to let her move in with me. I haven't even convinced Lindsay to live with me yet. Even then, it'll make her suspicious if I offer to let her friend move in.

"Are you in danger if you stay a little longer?" I don't want to make her stay if she's not safe. I'll figure it out even if it means outing this entire scheme to Lindsay.

"No, I just don't want to be around this life anymore." Her voice is so small. Very un-Tenille-like. It makes me feel awful to see her so vulnerable.

"Let me put this fire out first and then I'll figure out a way to get you out. Can you handle it a little longer?"

"Yeah, I can wait. Let's make sure Lindsay is safe first and then we'll worry about me."

CHAPTER 22
LINDSAY

It's moving day. I can't believe I let Rhett talk me into moving in with him. That's a lie. It wasn't difficult to convince me after somebody broke into my house.

He called Tenille and asked her to dig into the threat against me. Ram told her I needed to go away. I didn't need to disappear, but I needed to be far enough away I was no longer a threat to their operations. I had to quit my job.

I called Snyder and quit, effective immediately. It did not surprise him in the least. He told me I'd be missed and wished me luck. He sounded relieved, like he wouldn't miss me because I was more of a pain in the ass than anything.

I've come to terms with my decision. I worked my ass off to get to where I was, but at what cost? My devotion to my job could have cost me my life. My only regret is Kody.

He's probably wondering why I abandoned him. The thought breaks my heart. I hope his new handler takes good care of him.

I've spent the last few days packing up my bedroom and my more personal items. Tenille has been coming over and helping to get my kitchen and living room packed.

I never did anything with the spare room. The only things in there were a few boxes I had never unpacked from my last move. Everything is ready to go, to merge my life with Rhett's.

Rhett has enlisted the help of his older brother, Trent. I haven't spent much time with him. He doesn't come around often.

Their sister, Kelly, is sweet as pie and someone I could become close friends with. I see her often since she works out of Rhett's house. She's warned me Trent wasn't as friendly. His wife can be jealous and makes it hard for him to socialize, so he puts off a "don't fuck with me" demeanor.

I'm sitting on my porch steps with a cup of hot tea when they pull up. I really miss my coffee in the morning, but the smell of it makes me nauseated. I think it's been the most depressing part of this pregnancy. Coffee used to be one of my favorite scents. My hope is I'll be able to drink it again in a few weeks, once my second trimester comes around and I'm not dealing with this dreadful morning sickness.

This is the first time I've been alone in quite a while. I had to convince Rhett I'd be fine on my own for a couple of hours. He needed to pick up his brother and the trailer, and it was easier for me to drive down in my truck so I could get some last-minute packing done before everybody arrived. He was reluctant but agreed. Our codependent behavior as of late cannot be healthy in the long run.

The boys pull up in Rhett's truck with a gooseneck trailer hitched inside the bed. We'll load all my furniture onto the trailer. Since Rhett's house is already nicely furnished, I'll store my stuff in his garage for the time being. There's an apartment above the garage he's been slowly remodeling. Once it's complete, my furnishings will go in there, and we'll use it as a guest house or something.

Tenille arrives a few minutes behind Rhett and Trent in her old Honda. Her eyes are bugging out of her head when Trent steps into view.

I can't say I blame her. He's a good-looking man, taller than Rhett by an inch but with the same build. His hair is blond with a slight wave and is long enough to twine around a finger.

I laugh out loud when she fans herself. Rhett wraps his arms around me as I rise from the stairs to greet him.

"What's got you laughing this morning?" he asks and presses a sweet kiss to my lips.

"Look at Tenille. She's got the hots for your brother," I say, laughing more when she pulls her shirt away from her chest as if she's overcome with heat. Maybe she has.

"Oh, Lord, she's going to be hitting on him all day. I'd better warn him."

"No! Don't. Let him find out the hard way. It'll be entertaining to watch the drama unfold. I won't have anything else to do since you won't let me help load my own shit. I'm pregnant, not helpless," I say exasperatedly.

He and Tenille ganged up on me yesterday when we finished the last of my packing. Neither of them thought it was a good idea to let me lift anything. I understand I should probably set some limits, but not helping at all seems unreasonable. I can help with the smaller things and sit back and admire the flex of Rhett's muscles as he deals with the heavier stuff. Seems like a solid plan to me, but I'm the only one who thinks so.

For some reason, Tenille has become oddly invested in my pregnancy. She's excited and wants to be included in everything. I drew the line at her being present for the first ultrasound. I wasn't comfortable with my friend watching them stick a long probe up my vag. It was not pleasant.

I never thought Tenille liked kids. She always wrinkles her nose in disgust at the mention of babies, but her excitement for my baby is genuine. I'm sure of it.

Rhett gives me another quick kiss and rubs his hand over the slight swell of my belly before saying, "Okay, I won't warn him, but I'm warning you, if she tries to molest him or something, I can't be held responsible for how he responds to it. He's not as easygoing as I am."

We hold hands as he leads me to the end of the trailer. Trent is dropping the gate to create a ramp and unstrapping a large dolly they brought to make loading my furniture easier. Tenille inserts herself into the situation to ensure she gets to take part in the introductions.

"Trent, you remember Lindsay, and this is her best friend, Tenille. Ladies, this is my big brother, Trent."

I reach my hand out toward him, sensing he's not much of a hugger but figure he won't turn down a handshake. I was wrong. He nods in our direction, grunts a barely audible "hey," and gets back to what he was doing.

I drop my hand and let out a nervous laugh. That was awkward. I turn toward Rhett, unsure of how to respond to his brother's brush-off.

He shrugs with a sheepish smile. "Don't worry about it. I think he's going through something at home. He'll warm up eventually. Let's get to loading. I want to get as much done as we can before it gets too hot."

Trent has already made his way into my house with the hand truck, so we follow.

An hour later, my bedroom and living room furniture has been loaded onto the trailer. All that remains is most of the boxes and my small dinette set.

We decide now would be a good time to take a break and sit on the floor of the empty living room. I get them all cold bottles of water and hand them out, then sit next to Rhett and lay my head on his shoulder.

Trent seems to have lightened up a bit and is carrying a conversation with Rhett about the repairs to the apartment above his garage.

"How much longer do you think it'll be before it's finished?" Trent asks.

Rhett takes a healthy swig from his water bottle. He bounces his head back and forth in thought as he swallows before replying. "Probably another six months at the rate I'm going. I'd like to get it done before the baby comes though, so I'm going to have to knuckle down and knock it out."

Trent contemplates for a moment. "Do you need some help? I could come over on the weekends and after work."

"What about spending time with Rachel and Law Man?" Rhett asks.

"Don't worry about that. I could always bring Lawson with me, and he could hang out with Lindsay if he gets in our way. I'm sure Rachel would like the time to herself anyway."

Rhett turns toward me. He takes my hand in his and settles them between his outstretched legs. "Would you mind if Lawson hung out with you? I could really use Trent's help to get the apartment ready so I can focus on getting the nursery set up next."

"Of course, I don't mind. I'd love to spend time with your nephew. It'll be good practice for when this little one crashes our party." I rub circles on my small bump.

Tenille, never one to keep quiet for long, injects herself into the conversation. "What's this apartment you speak of?"

"It's above my detached garage. You'll see it when we go to unload all of this." Rhett gestures around us vaguely.

"Do you have somebody lined up to move into it?" Tenille asks curiously.

"We hadn't planned to rent it out," Rhett says. "I thought we might use it for guest quarters. Why do you ask?"

I'm a little surprised to see Tenille so interested in the apartment. She is still living above the bar where she works. I wonder if there is something wrong and if she's looking for another place to live. I decide not to ask in front of Trent and Rhett.

"You're taking my best friend and soon-to-be niece or nephew. Maybe I want the opportunity to be close to them." Tenille tries to sound nonchalant about the whole thing, but I detect a little sadness in her words. "I'm going to go smoke and then I think we should finish up."

Tenille walks out the front door, and Trent gets up without a word and makes his way down the hall to the bathroom. Rhett and I go into my bedroom to gather my clothes from my closet to lay in the back seat of his truck.

We aren't in the bedroom long when we hear Trent's loud voice echo through the mostly empty house.

"What the fuck?"

Rhett and I are looking at each other knowingly when we hear Tenille's full-bellied laugh.

We make it to the hallway in time to see Trent step out of the bathroom door. He uses his size to intimidate Tenille, and she backs up into the wall, looking up at his face. Her expression is a mixture of mirth and trepidation. She bites the corner of her bottom lip, trying to hide her smile.

"Who the fuck walks in on somebody in the bathroom on purpose? Especially somebody you just met!" Trent says through clenched teeth.

Tenille has the good sense to wince slightly. "Well..." She pauses a beat. "My curiosity got the better of me. I know how big Rhett's cock is, and you're built bigger than he is, so I had to know if you were as nicely proportioned as your brother." Tenille shrugs like it's no big deal, like her reasoning is totally acceptable.

Trent's eyes widen, and he looks at Rhett and me with a look that asks: "What the fuck?"

Tenille adds to the shitshow. "In case you were wondering, you're longer, although I think Rhett might have you beat in girth. They're both really nice dicks either way. I'd be happy to take either of them for a ride," she says, in all seriousness.

I throw my head back and laugh. This girl is too much sometimes. Rhett laughs too, just not as enthusiastically as me.

"I'm married," Trent says irritably.

"She's a very lucky lady," Tenille says.

Trent scrubs his hand against his face a few times and mutters something sounding like "she doesn't think so" as he walks away. He grabs a stack of boxes from the kitchen and heads for the front door.

I rush ahead to open the door for him. I feel like I need to smooth things over, so I say, "I'm sorry about her. She did the same thing to Rhett the first day she met him. We should've warned you she might try to take a peek. I really am sorry, Trent. I'll talk to her and make sure she doesn't try anything else, and thank you for helping today."

He shakes his head and continues out the door to load the boxes. I really hope Tenille's stunt hasn't turned Rhett's brother off. They're close, and I don't want my friend to be a reason they grow apart. I'm afraid this might keep him from getting to know me. He might judge me by my friend's actions. I love the girl like a sister, but it doesn't mean I condone all her wildly inappropriate behaviors.

I'm still holding onto the door when Rhett comes by with a couple more boxes. He leans over and kisses me sweetly. "Don't worry about it. I'll talk to him. He's got a stick up his ass today. He'll laugh about all this tomorrow."

Tenille rides with me in my truck to Rhett's house. We figured it was best to keep her away from Trent as much as possible. I thought it would be a good opportunity to grill her a little on why she was so interested in the garage apartment, but she beats me to it with a question of her own.

"Are you nervous to be moving in with Rhett so early in your relationship? It's only been what, a month?" Tenille asks seriously.

It's strange because most of the words that come out of her mouth are lewd or sarcastic. For as long as I've known her, she's never had to take anything seriously. She doesn't pay rent. I think her only bills are insurance and her phone. She doesn't have the responsibilities most people in their late twenties do, so her maturity level seems to be stuck somewhere around sixteen.

"I'm scared shitless," I say honestly. "It seems our entire relationship has been on fast forward though, so why not this too? If we're going to have a relationship and raise this baby together, we both need to be all in at the same time. I started out being all in, while he was trying to keep things casual, and then I gave up when he was coming around. It's time we both get on the same page and figure out what it means to be a family since that's what we're going to be in twenty-eight weeks."

"I don't think you have anything to worry about. Rhett seems great for you, and he's going to be an amazing father. Just don't close yourself off to him, because you'll be shutting the door on something truly amazing."

Where in the world is this coming from? I figured she'd be the one telling me to keep playing the field instead of settling down. Enough about me. I'm getting to the bottom of this introspective version of my best friend. "What's going on with you, girl? Why were you asking about the garage apartment?" I glance her way for a second before returning my eyes to the road.

"Lindsay, I'm not sure if you've put two and two together yet, but I live above the bar, owned by a member of the gang that tried to kill you. Ram and I have always had an understanding. He couldn't have an opinion about our friendship. You're all I've got when he's not around. I think he understood that despite you being the last person he'd want me to be best friends with, you'd take care of me if I ever needed you to. You're good for me, so he pretended you weren't the one shutting down his club brother's main income." She says all of this to the window with her hands knotted in her lap. "But I can't be around that anymore. The lines have blurred way too much."

My brows pinch together as I realize she's right. I hadn't put it together. I've been so wrapped up in my own shit, I didn't stop to think about how my career might affect her. When I first got the job at the prison, she and I had been friends for about a year. She was living above the bar, but we never hung out there. She always came to my place. After we turned twenty-one and we started going to the bar, I never met Ram or any of the other members of the gang. When Tenille invited me to come drink and listen to a cover band for the first time, I'd asked about running into the guys, and she'd assured me she'd never invite me if any of them were going to be there.

I keep having these realizations of how good of a friend Tenille's been to me and how selfish I've been. I'm disgusted with myself. She did everything she could to get me to loosen up and have a little fun when all I was focused on was working myself to death. I had a one-track mind, set on making it into K-9. Once I made it happen, my sights were on being the best.

While I was only worried about myself, Tenille was worried about me. She protected me, and all I ever did was take her for granted. I haven't even met the man who has been her pseudo-boyfriend for at least as long as I've known her. I know nothing about where she comes from or who her family is. I asked early on, and she shut me down by saying Ram and I are the only family she'll ever need and then distracted me with something else. I should have pushed harder. I could've made more of an effort to learn about her life before we met and, hell, even after we became friends.

"Tenille, I'm sorry I've been such a shitty friend to you. If you really want to move out of your apartment, I'll talk to Rhett. I'm sure he'll let you move into the garage apartment when it's finished, and if you feel you need to leave sooner than that, I'll ask him about letting you move into the house with us in the meantime."

"I'll take you up on the apartment but not on the room in the house. I'd be too tempted to come join in when I hear the two of you fucking down the hall," she says with a sassy smile.

"Ah, there's my girl. I wondered what happened to my favorite jezebel. Seriously though, I'd rather you live with us than be in a bad situation longer than you have to."

"It's really not a bad situation. He doesn't mistreat me or anything. It's an environment I don't want to be in anymore. I can't associate with people who tried to kill you. I'm also going to need to look for a job. I can't keep tending bar there." She has a point. I'm going to ask Rhett about that too. Maybe he has a place in his company for her.

GREENLIGHT

"Okay, I'll just ask about the apartment then." When I glance at her, she gives me a grateful smile. I decide it's time I ask what I should've asked years ago. "Tenille, will you tell me how you met Ram?"

She turns toward me, her expression full of apprehension. I lock eyes with her as long as I can before I need to look back to the road, hoping she sees how much I care about her even though I've been terrible at proving it.

She takes in a huge breath and lets it out slowly through her nose before she finally speaks. "I ran away when I was sixteen. Ram found me and took me in. He gives me a safe place to live and makes sure I always have anything I need. In return, I make sure his bar doesn't burn down and keeps making money while he's out doing whatever it is he does with the club."

My heart sinks to my stomach. She has sex with him. I knew he was older than her, but now I wonder by how much. Does she have some form of Stockholm Syndrome? What kind of grown man takes in a teenage girl and has sex with her? Not a good one, that's for sure.

"I know what you're thinking, and you can stop. He didn't touch me until I was much older, and I was the one to initiate it. He also didn't let any of the guys touch me either. He took me away from a life of hell and gave me so much better. None of those guys have ever treated me badly. The only reason I'm leaving them is because of what they did to you. You should also know Ram had nothing to do with what happened, and when he found out, he shut that shit down. This was something being done off the table. Only certain members were in on it. Nobody will come after you again without severe retaliation from him." She takes my hand off the steering wheel and holds it in hers for a second. "You're safe, babe."

Relief and gratitude pour from my eyes. It's been in the back of my mind I might never truly be free from the threat of the Zona MC. Once again, it's Tenille who has saved my ass—not the government I worked for but my rough-around-the-edges best friend.

"Thank you," I whisper as I wipe tears from my cheeks. "Part of me is so happy you're ready to step away from that lifestyle. But after hearing Ram takes good care of you, it makes me feel guilty you might give up somebody who means a lot to you."

She shrugs. "Don't feel guilty. Ram has always sheltered me from so much of his life because he didn't want me to get too deep. We talked when he was home last, and he agreed it's time for me to move on. I'm not giving him up for you. I'm taking control of my own life."

CHAPTER 23
RHETT

I'm so fucking nervous.

Shawn called and invited us to his show in Vegas. It sparked an idea in my head I couldn't turn loose of. I ran my idea by him, and he took it and ran. Told me not to worry about a thing, he'd have it all handled.

So here we are, Lindsay and I, along with Trent and Tenille, watching my cousin sing his heart out from backstage. My palms are sweaty, my heart is pounding, and I feel like I could puke.

Lindsay dances in front of me, brushing her sweet ass up against me every chance she gets, making my jeans fit a little tighter. I'm going to embarrass myself in a few minutes if she doesn't stop. I grab her hips, spin her to face me, and slam our lips together.

As Shawn wraps up his song, I break away and the stage lights dim. A roadie taps my shoulder and hands me a guitar by its strap so I can slip it over my head as I hustle on stage to take my place on a stool next to Shawn.

The lights come back up and Shawn addresses the crowd, introducing me to them and explaining he and I are going to do a song together. When I look over at my girl, she stands with her hands over her mouth, in complete shock. I've kept this a secret from her. I smile and shoot her a wink. She drops her hands, a smile lighting up her entire face, and blows me a kiss.

I strum the opening chords to "So Help Me Girl" by Joe Diffie. As I sing the lyrics, with Shawn singing harmony, I turn slightly so I can watch as she stands there looking beautiful, with tears shining in her eyes. Tenille stands at her side, hugging her arm as though Lindsay would be a puddle on the floor without her support. I pour everything I feel for her into every word.

When the final chord rings out, the entire arena breaks into loud cheers as my girl comes running onto the stage. Shawn grabs the guitar from me just in time as Lindsay crashes into my chest. I wrap my arms around her and lift her feet off the ground for a second before I set her down and drop to one knee.

Holding a diamond ring in one hand and Lindsay's left hand in the other, I open my mouth to speak but Shawn steps in and stops me. "Hang on, brother, you need a microphone. I know the good folks here tonight want to hear this."

Lindsay giggles nervously behind her hand. The one in mine trembles slightly, so I give it a squeeze and a little shake. "Keep your eyes right here. It's just you and me, baby," I say as Shawn sets a mic stand in my face, causing my voice to boom loudly over the speakers.

He laughs and gestures, allowing me to continue while the crowd cheers me on.

"Lindsay, baby, from the moment I laid eyes on you, my heart knew what my mind refused to believe. You're my forever. I know our story is just beginning, but I never want to see it end. Lindsay Rose Lanier, will you marry me?"

The noise level of the arena becomes deafening when Lindsay nods. I slide the ring onto her finger and rise to my full height. I hold my fiancée tight against my chest, bury my face in her hair, kiss the side of her neck, and I whisper, "I love you," in her ear.

Shawn interrupts our intimate moment, wrapping both of us in a bear hug and screaming, "She said yes, y'all!" into the microphone over my shoulder. My ears ring from the level of excitement palpable around us.

STEVIE LEE

I lead my girl off the stage, where we're greeted by my brother and my girl's hot mess of a best friend. Trent pulls me in for a congratulatory bro hug, and Tenille and Lindsay share a tearful hug.

The band plays the lead-in for Shawn's next song when we hear him speak to the crowd. "This next song is for those crazy lovebirds. I'm sure this song will describe the next few hours perfectly." He laughs through the first few words of the song about getting it on in the bed of his truck. He's as crude as Tenille. I swear those two were made for each other if either one would settle down.

We finish the show with my arms around my little family. My hands rub the baby bump that protects my daughter as she dances along to the throbbing bass of the band. I'm here with the most important people in the world to me, minus my parents and sister, and I can't help but chuckle and shake my head when I say, "I'm the luckiest son of a bitch in the world."

With my lips against Lindsay's ear, I whisper, "I've got a surprise for you." Lindsay turns in my arms on our bed. Her cheek has pressure lines and is slightly reddened from her pillow. She's adorable in her groggy state. Our baby kicks against my hand hard enough for Lindsay to wince. I chuckle at her expense. I swear this little girl is going to be a boxer if her mama's reactions to her jabs are any indication.

Lindsay knocks her knuckles against my chest. "Don't laugh at me. It isn't funny. She nailed me in the bladder. I almost pissed the bed," she whines, her voice raspy from sleep.

I laugh harder, watching her roll out of bed on her way to the bathroom. She went from barely showing to watermelon status—overnight, it seems. I've loved every minute of her ever-changing body.

My cock stirs to life. The sway of her hips as she waddles away is a whole new level of sexy I didn't know existed. I mentally talk myself down. Now is not the time to be turned on. My phone chimes with a second text, alerting me to the arrival of her surprise. I can't wait to see her face light up when she sees what I've done.

I hand her a bra when she emerges from the bathroom. Her boobs have almost doubled in size during her pregnancy. She's a little self-conscious of them, and I know she'll appreciate this gesture once she steps outside in the presence of another person.

The bra dangles from her fingers between us, her expression one of annoyance. "Why are you giving me this?"

"Trust me," I say with an arrogant smirk.

"They're sore. I don't want to shove them into this damn thing."

"You can take it off as soon as you get your surprise, and I'll massage them for you." I wiggle my brows at her suggestively. "But I promise you're going to want to have it on for this."

She rolls her eyes at me but pulls her shirt over her head to put the bra on.

When we're both dressed, I take her hand and lead her through the house toward the front door.

As we step out onto the porch, a guy named Payne approaches with Kody on a leash.

Kody sees her first. His paws dance with excitement against the grass. He whines and barks, finally catching Lindsay's attention. She shrieks and runs down the porch steps, falling to her knees in front of her partner. I watch her with the biggest smile on my face, even though she's completely forgotten about me.

Kody jumps into her arms, knocking her off balance. Lindsay crashes onto her back with Kody wrapped tightly in her arms. My heart plummets to my stomach, worried about the huge dog crushing her pregnant belly, but her laughter sets me at ease. His body vibrates with the effort to hold still as she clings to him.

She rolls to her side, dumping Kody onto the ground, and rises to her knees, scrubbing her fingers through his thick fur. She coos at him like a baby as he licks her face affectionately, soaking up her praise. I'm happy to watch her in this moment. Most of our time together was tainted with fear. She's slowly relaxing and becoming a less-stressed version of herself, but right now, she's happier than I have ever seen her—which includes when I asked her to marry me. It's nice to know marrying me doesn't make her as happy as having her beloved dog. I should be jealous, but I'm not. I'd do anything to keep this smile on her beautiful face. I know she's missed him immensely, and soon enough, she'll be looking for my affections too. At least, I hope she will.

I shake Payne's hand, thanking him for bringing Kody. I know he and Lindsay didn't really get along, so I let him off the hook so he can leave. The only reason he's here is because Kody can't be led by just anybody. He must be with a trained handler.

I'm lucky to have the connection with Keith. Otherwise, I wouldn't have been able to arrange for Kody's retirement and adoption. It took some sweet-talking on my end, but I finally got the department to relent. The stipulation was Payne had to be the one to turn Kody over to Lindsay. I expected a hefty adoption fee; I can only imagine what the cost of training and caring for these dogs could be, but I was surprised when they only charged me a dollar.

After watching Lindsay and Kody roll around and play for a while, I approach so I can meet the beast who has my girl's heart. When I get within a few feet of them, Kody steps between Lindsay and me and leans his weight against her, pushing her away from me. A growl rumbles deep in his chest. I come to a halt. This might be a problem. If this dog won't let me near Lindsay, it's going to be a sad day.

Lindsay says a word in a language I don't understand, and Kody's demeanor changes... marginally. He's no longer growling, but he's alert and assessing me.

Lindsay's laughter brings my attention away from Kody.

"What's so funny?" I ask, not understanding how her dog wanting to eat me could be so hilarious.

"He's been trained anybody in orange is the enemy."

I look down, and sure enough, I grabbed a pair of orange basketball shorts and a white T-shirt. I look like an inmate. "Should I go change?"

She nods, only half paying attention to me. She spent every day for years trusting this dog with her life. These last few months have been terrifying, and she's had to get through them without him. I tried to fill that role, and I think I did. I can tell though, no matter how hard I try to protect her, she will always feel safest with him by her side.

When I step back out onto the porch in clothing that makes me look less like a convict and more like a civilian, I find Lindsay lying on her back in the grass staring up at the clouds. Kody is against her side with one paw across the underside of her belly. His chin hovers over the bump as his eyes scan the landscape, looking for any potential threat to his master.

His head cocks to the side, ears perked as he drops his gaze. Her stomach shifts in a large wave as the baby rolls around. He nudges with his nose, sniffing rapidly, trying to figure out what is going on. Lindsay lays her hand gently on his head, and he lays it on her. His eyes still dart around, but he's content with his head bumping up and down with the baby's movements.

I snap a quick picture with my phone. I want to show my daughter the day she got her protector. I'm sure Kody will warm up to me quickly when he realizes we share the same goal in caring for our girls.

EPILOGUE
LINDSAY

We're exactly one week from the wedding. We're having a small ceremony with our closest family and friends in our backyard under a beautiful arch Rhett's dad, Ray, built for the occasion. I can't believe we've made it to this place. I feel like each trimester of this pregnancy marks another life event.

At the end of the first trimester, I moved in with Rhett.

At the end of the second, he asked me to marry him.

And now that we're ending the third, I'm about to become his wife.

Wife. Mother.

Those two titles are about to be mine, two words I didn't allow myself to even consider until I met Rhett. They excite me more than anything else ever has.

Rhett's mom and sister have decided I need some sexy lingerie for my wedding night. I don't see the point. I'm the size of a house. Adding satin and lace won't help my cause.

I'm in the mall with them anyway. Kelly and I are browsing through racks of baby dolls, since they're about the only thing that will fit over my belly. Charlotte, his mom, is off browsing around, in her own little world.

Kelly is holding up a pretty black chemise with purple accents when we hear Charlotte shouting our names from across the store.

We turn and find her holding up a flamingo G-string in one hand and an elephant in the other.

"Kell, we should buy these for Rhett and Trent!" she shouts.

I burst into laughter. The image of those two big burly men wearing those ridiculous G-strings is too much. I can't get a hold of myself.

I cross my ankles, trying to keep from peeing myself. I'm hunched over, holding onto a table covered in panties to keep from falling over.

Kelly is not laughing. Her face is bright red, and her hands are on top of her head. "Mom! No! Put those down, now!"

"But they're cute! It would be funny to get them for the boys!" Poor Charlotte is dead serious. She doesn't see how inappropriate it is to buy her sons underwear that highlight their… manhood in animal form.

Inappropriate or not, I find it hilarious.

Just as I think I can catch my breath from laughing so much, I feel an odd pop. I pause, wondering what in the world it was when I feel a trickle.

Oh shit, I think my water broke. Either that or I peed myself after I stopped laughing.

"Hey, Kelly?" My voice is small and shaky. She doesn't hear me. She's still berating her mother over the T-back britches. "Uh, Kelly, I think my water broke," I say, a little louder this time, finally catching her attention.

"Oh, fuck! Mom put the man thongs down. We gotta go! You're about to be a grandma again."

THE END

THANK YOU for reading GREENLIGHT!
Get Trent and Tenille's story in *Caution*, now available!

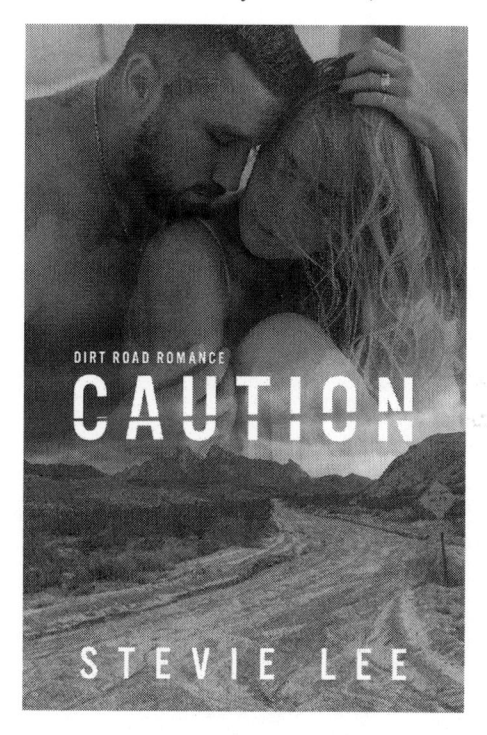

CAUTION: HEARTBREAK AHEAD

I never cared what anybody thought of me.

I lived a wild and carefree life until the outlaw motorcycle club I called family put a bounty on my best friend's head.

When I decide to leave that life behind, I'm blindsided by Trent Caraway, a single dad who despises me.

Trent and I are complete opposites. We'd never work. Being a stepmom and going to bed with the same man every night doesn't interest me.

Until one drunken conversation reveals deeper possibilities. My brash attitude and sexual exploits are the only armor I have to protect myself from one truth: Trent has the power to hurt me if I let him.

ABOUT THE AUTHOR

Stevie Lee is a rare Arizona native. She married her best friend's older brother, who also happened to be the boy next door, a month after graduation. She's the proud mama to her two kids and recently adopted two pit bull-yorkie pups (yes, you read that right!).

When she's not writing or mothering, Stevie is a country music junkie and can't wait for concerts to be a thing again. In the meantime, you can find her sewing or curled up with a good book and a margarita.

www.stevieleewrites.com
https://www.facebook.com/AuthorStevieLee
https://www.instagram.com/stevieleewrites/
https://www.facebook.com/groups/283530696077229

Made in United States
Orlando, FL
09 February 2024